MW00804340

Stitches and *Brushes*

"I LOVED this book and did not want it to end…It has mystery, adventure, romance and fun. This is a book of guilty pleasure."

—Reader Review, *Stitches*

"I can honestly say everyone is in for a real treat! Finally we have a new and delightful mystery writer!"

—Reader Review, *Stitches*

"She had me in the first chapter. I loved it and recommend it to everyone who likes a good story. Simple as that. Suspend all disbelief and simply enjoy the ride!"

—Reader Review, *Stitches*

"*Stitches* is a treasure of simple story telling at its best…Courtney's ability to describe her characters and the places they live and visit is second to none, in my book. I can think of many lauded authors who should have her ability…Courtney had touched a place in my heart with her characters."

—Reader Review, *Stitches*

"The way she describes the painting absolutely brings it to life in my mind's eye. I enjoy being transported into a life of magic, fun, and adventure with Courtney Pierce leading the way."

—Reader Review, *Brushes*

"The story telling is first rate…suspend any need for reality and just suppose it's all possible. What a fun concept. Thanks, Courtney for a fun ride…couldn't put it down…finished reading it around 4 a.m."

—Reader Review, *Brushes*

"All the characters are well developed and that is what really makes this book for me…definitely worth the time to not miss any of the details. All I can say is, I want an immortal dog too now!"

—Reader Review, *Brushes*

Riffs

Courtney Pierce

Windtree Press
818 SW 3rd Avenue #221-2218
Portland, OR 97204-2405

Windtree Press
818 SW 3rd Avenue #221-2218
Portland, OR 97204-2405

Cover Photo:

Sara Sami

Used by Permission

ISBN-10: 0988917521
ISBN-13: 978-0-9889175-2-1

DEDICATION

To my husband, Wayne, who hears the music all the time.

"When you hear music, after it's over, it's gone, in the air. You can never capture it again."

—Eric Dolphy

ACKNOWLEDGMENTS

Thanks, as always, go to my husband, Wayne, and to my entire family for their support of my literary journey.

My editor, Kristin Thiel, is a delight. Her ability to remain objective while being a cat lover is remarkable.

Thank you to Helen Dupre, Christina Dupre, Debbie Gerber, Carole Florian and Annette Beck. As first readers, your generous time and suggestions were greatly appreciated.

Special thanks go to Jennifer Lauck, best-selling author, teacher, mentor, and motivator extraordinaire. My months of intense study at the Attic Institute became a food group for nourishing my imagination and refining my writing craft. There's no one right or wrong way to tell a story, only the quest to ensure the words don't get in the way.

As a new addition to the Windtree Press family, I would like to thank Maggie Lynch and all of my fellow authors for welcoming me with open arms. Windtree's theme is "books with a heart," and they have lived up to those words.

Lastly, I am grateful for my involvement in NIWA (Northwest Independent Writers Association) and the Attic Institute. Both organizations offer a supportive environment for writers who want to make their books the best they can be.

CHAPTER 1

Keep Your Paws Inside

Life seemed different with having a choice to become immortal. The final possibility changed how Jean Collins viewed today— this minute, this second. Flickers of warm sunlight bounced off the Willamette River as the 1963 Thunderbird convertible purred down River Road in Milwaukie, a quiet suburb on the southeast side of Portland, Oregon. Driving this car was like flying in a turquoise rocket ship. Spring wouldn't be this special if azaleas and rhodo-dendrons blossomed all year long.

An option at the end of natural life forced Jean and her husband, Spence, to do some serious planning about what was important in the here and now, as well as dreaming about what was possible in the life beyond. After careful thought about an immortal life, Spence leaned toward mortality because he was convinced the best music had already been written and recorded on vinyl. She wasn't so sure. But whatever they chose when the time came, they had to be in sync.

The older she and Spence got, the more youth seemed to fill them from the inside out. In their opinion, youth was not wasted on the young because life's possibilities were still in front of them. At fifty-three and sixty-one, the last thing they wanted was to retire— from life, that is. They had both walked away from their careers— Jean from years of corporate politics and deal making in the Broadway entertainment industry and Spence from directing a community college education program—but after that, all getting older meant was doing something different and break from convention. As baby boomers, Jean and Spence were finally understanding the sixties belief they'd come of age with: "anything's possible" really meant something to them at this stage of life. Jean's customized license plate read TBS-R-GO, named after her and Spence's favorite sixties space puppet show, *Thunderbirds Are Go*. That was Spence's idea after they'd inherited the Thunderbird from Mary Coulter, the woman who'd given them way more than just earthly possessions (in the form of her family home in Richmond, Virginia, an Arts and Crafts bungalow in Portland where she had lived, significant investments, and, of course, the amazing T-Bird).

Ever since Jean had found the ancient magical fabric in an old trunk at Mary Coulter's estate sale last September, life had gone from ordinary to extraordinary. The unexplainable had become an everyday occurrence. The fabric had the power to make people immortal, and in the span of these ten months, Jean and Spence had watched that happen, become friends with immortals, and thwarted living bad guys.

Magic, and the good and the bad that traveled with it, was not their only preoccupation. The renovation of Mary Coulter's house in Portland was Jean's project in the coming months. Spence's dream would soon be realized with the opening of Not Fade Away, a vintage vinyl store, with his friend and business partner Bill Flannery. Bill and his wife, Linda, were friends first, business partners second. The grand opening was going to be celebrated with a jazz festival in downtown Milwaukie, coming up in only three weeks.

Jean glanced in the rearview mirror and smiled. Their adopted immortal dog, Wiley, loved to ride in the T-Bird. He sat in the back seat with his paws on the window frame, his face to the wind. A spray of sparkles blew from the flaps of his ears, and with the top down, he'd found his heaven.

"Keep your paws inside," Jean warned. "You're a good boy, Wiley. We're on our way home to hear Spence on the radio. Who wants to see Mycroft?" Wiley wagged his tail and turned in a circle, tendrils of wispy haze chasing after him.

If anything could get Wiley more excited than a ride in the Thunderbird, it was spending time with Mycroft, her and Spence's twenty-two-pound Maine Coon cat. Those two were like peas and carrots. And when the temperature dropped below fifty degrees, as it did on most spring nights in Oregon, Wiley and Mycroft could be found entwined by the gas fireplace. That is, unless they were visiting Doc, Mary Coulter's adoptive father, inside his portrait in the living room.

Dr. Beaumont Gaines became immortal with the magical fabric in 1931. He and his whole immortal family—his wife, Charlotte; Mary Coulter; and Birdie and Jess, the housekeeper and handyman—lived in the Victorian home in Richmond, Virginia, now run by a lovely pair of mortals as a bed-and-breakfast. Jean and Spence considered them their own family. Wiley, Doc's immortal black Labrador, had wormed his way into their world and their hearts. The dog now spent more time in their house in Milwaukie than in Richmond. And he loved his rides in the car.

The power of the magical fabric had to be secured after Jean and Spence transformed Mary Coulter. Pursued by thieves and scared at what harm the fabric could do if released to the greater public or to people with ill intentions, Jean and Spence had donated the fabric to the Cairo Museum. The relic belonged to Egypt. The important artifact from Nefertari's tomb was now in the care of Anhur Kumar, the museum's executive director, and was on display inside an alarmed Plexiglas case. Its secrets were still hidden from the world, but the magic lingered behind—inside of her and Spence. Contact with the fabric had awakened their sense of touch with the ability to see the history of Mary's heirlooms. Or maybe the heirlooms themselves were magical. They couldn't tell.

Jean filled her lungs with piney air as she adjusted her oversize black sunglasses. The fringe of the long, turquoise scarf around her head stretched and waved toward the backseat. With his wife's blond pageboy tucked away, Spence called the look her "menopausal Jackie O." Jean used to change her hair—color, cut, or both, with each acquisition or merger in her corporate job. She had felt the need to mark each new era. Now she stuck with her favorite look. Before, she'd needed to exact that bit of control in her otherwise chaotic life. Now, though her life was equally as topsy-turvy, sometimes even with less logic than the corporate world had offered, she was truly happy, and having fun—and somehow she felt more in control than ever. Perhaps because she just threw her arms in the air and rode with it…

The button on the CD player drew her forefinger. The speakers sprang to life with the lope-along beat of the Clash's *Rudy Can't Fail.* She tapped her aqua, kid-leather driving gloves on the steering wheel, the size of a hula-hoop used by small dogs to perform tricks. The vintage gloves were required accoutrement for keeping the visions of the car's history at bay. If Jean's skin touched the car, she was subject to witnessing the scenes that had transpired in and around the car over its lifespan. Holding the wheel with her bare hands was a no-no while driving. The visions were lovely and interesting, sometimes sad, but she had living and driving to do of her own. Getting lost in someone else's memories didn't seem healthy.

Jean pressed the gas. She had to get home. In twenty-seven minutes, Spence would be promoting Not Fade Away's grand-opening concert on Rick Rakin's Sunday jazz radio show on KRIFF. The store was a fifty-year dream for Spence, the culmination of decades of passionate collecting that had needed a nudge of magic to become something tangible. Since meeting the great jazz musician Legs Flanders, who had given him the harmonica once played by Muddy Waters, Spence had been downright inspired.

The publicity from the radio interview would put the store on the map, without a doubt, but Spence was equally excited just to be talking about music. He could shoot out obscure, juicy bits of music trivia with the speed and accuracy of a nail gun. On point—every time.

And while Spence and Bill channeled their nervous energy about the store opening into obsessive record spinning at the store— "Gotta listen to one more record, and then I'll be home!"—Jean was doing what she did best. She tapped the steering wheel in time to the music as her mind whirled through her to-do list: Bill had the inventory organized and priced; Spence had the musicians primed, with both logistics and enthusiasm; Linda had finalized the catering arrangements with Casa de Tamales; and Jean herself had the last duke-it-out with the city over permits for the tented stage. Press releases had been sent to media. Next up were the personal invitations to every friend they had in the Pacific Northwest. Even the mailman made the list. She had expected, by now, to have heard from Legs Flanders. But since he was eighty-two, she didn't want to get her hopes up that Legs would be willing to make the trip from Washington, DC, just to play his harmonica for the grand finale.

Home. "Home!" Jean announced to Wiley as she rolled the T-Bird into the garage. She pulled off her gloves and sunglasses and set them in the glove compartment. She grabbed her purse and bag of Mycroft's prescription food for senior cats and shepherded Wiley into the house. At the first step through the mudroom, Jean sensed she wasn't alone.

"Hey, hi, who's here?" she called out as she stepped into the kitchen. Wiley's thick toenails clacked on the bamboo floor ahead of her in his quest to find Mycroft. Their 1960s garden home offered an open, unobstructed view of three levels.

"All's fine," Birdie's voice said from the upstairs catwalk. "I thought you'd be home soon." She clapped her hands. "Wiley, you come here! We gotta go! Doc's gonna paddle your behind." Birdie, herself an immortal, was the housekeeper for the Gaines family. She couldn't get enough of Mycroft.

"Aren't you going to stick around to hear Spence on the radio?" Jean asked. The slight illumination around Birdie's full face and thick arms contrasted with her dark skin. The blue cornflowers on her yellow cotton dress accentuated her substantial waist and wide hips.

"I catch him. Not to worry. Jess gonna too, make no mistake."

"You're not here because of trouble with Mycroft, are you?"

"Goodness, no. I call him Fluffy. I don't know why you ever name him Mycroft. He ain't solvin' nothin', that cat. He order me around and stare out the window. He look left, and then he look right." Birdie chuckled. "Yes, ma'am, that all he do. I give him some crunchy things, but he don't eat 'em. Not hungry, I guess…"

"Odd. He's always hungry." Jean held up the bag of cat food.

"If he ain't sleepin', then he bossin'. He a funny one, orderin' me around like he do."

"Where is Mycroft, anyway?"

"On Doc's lap." Birdie blew out a breath through the gap in her otherwise perfect front teeth and lumbered down the stairs. With one scolding hand on her hip, she pointed to the portrait of Doc in the living room, the one painted by Dillon Davis, the gifted nineteen-year-old artist Jean and Spence had befriended during their adventure getting to know Mary Coulter's Richmond house. Really, Dillon had become so close with Jean and Spence that they considered him the son they never had. As a painter, he would have been a formidable contemporary of Caravaggio, had he lived in the late sixteenth century with the Italian master, but as a future art sleuth with the FBI, he would give the world's lost art a chance to go home.

Birdie clapped her hands. "Big Fluffy, you come outta there! Right now! Your momma's home."

Mycroft wasn't immortal, but he was full of magic. After lying on the enchanted fabric, he transformed a bird to immortality after it ran into the dining room's sliding glass door. After that, Mycroft discovered he could perform all kinds of magical shenanigans.

Inside the painting, Doc saluted Birdie with two fingers and scooted Mycroft's rump. With no hint of guilt—a conspicuously absent emotion in cats—Mycroft jumped out of the canvas, a trail of sparkles chasing him as his paws hit the carpet. Wiley raced up to the cat and licked the top of his head, his tail all the while wagging in a glittery fan.

"Thanks, Doc," Jean said. "I hope he's been good company."

"Doc's gettin' back at you for takin' Wiley for a ride. He tryin' to steal Fluffy," Birdie whispered from behind her hand. "Best be gettin' back. Never know what funny business go on when I'm away. C'mon, Wiley." The Labrador ran to Birdie and disappeared in mid-leap. Birdie, too, was gone. A wispy trail swirled in the same spot as the only evidence of their presence.

Glancing at her watch, Jean flinched and raced to the kitchen. She had only five minutes to remind Dillon to tune in the radio program. She picked up the phone and called his mobile.

"Hey there, Dillon. It's Jean. Don't forget Spence is on the jazz station, 97.2 FM, in a few minutes."

"Don't worry, I didn't forget. Recording it too. Working on Mary Coulter's portrait," Dillon said, sounding distracted and focused.

"How's Mary coming along?"

"Good, but slow. Her eyes are more complicated than I thought. I need her to appear in front of me for a while."

"Can't wait to see it. Birdie was just here. I should have asked her to send Mary to you. Think hard about her, Dillon. I bet she'll appear. Okay, gotta go."

Jean hung up and tuned in KRIFF on the stereo. "You ready for Daddy?"

Mycroft's bright green eyes gazed up at her like Spence really would come out of the stereo. He followed Jean's gaze to the speaker.

CHAPTER 2

Life Begins at 97.2 FM

Spence Collins sat across from Rick Rakin, the DJ for KRIFF 97.2 FM. The springs in the seat squeaked as he scooted the rolling chair in front of the fuzzy microphone. He pictured himself speaking into a huge bedroom slipper. The image helped to calm his nerves. Years of private passion, research, collecting, and spewing trivia had led to this: finally putting his money where his mouth was. The fantasy felt different than reality. Even at sixty-one, the same nervousness of taking a college exam bubbled to the surface. It was one thing to widen eyes with stories at a cocktail party but quite another matter to shoot them through the airwaves for public scrutiny.

The sixties oldies retrospectives on PBS popped into his head. He enjoyed seeing what his favorite rock stars looked like now in relation to the images burned into his memory. When pointing the finger at himself, Spence thought he measured up pretty well. His jeans were still the same size as when he was twenty. And while his dark hair had salt-and-peppered, Spence was thankful he still had all of it, even the cowlick on the crown. His dark Welsh eyes still had that touch of mischief, and his clear, deep voice had ensured a steady stream of dates. It had won over Jean thirty-five years ago.

The well-worn chair continued to groan as Spence swiveled right and left with anxious energy. Rick smiled, indicating he'd noticed the noise.

"Sorry."

"Just take it easy, man. You've got a radio voice," Rick assured. "My fans have been waiting for you. I've been fielding e-mails all week from record collectors who'll be coming to the event."

"No kidding?" Spence's chest puffed with newfound confidence. "Whatever you say. I'm ready." He slipped the headphones over his ears.

"Can't believe you're not sitting in my seat. You have got to do something important with that voice."

Spence cleared his throat.

The on-air light blinked a soft yellow glow. The letter *R* had been worn thin from something scratchy. The vintage equipment must have been rescued from a long-dead radio station, like everything else in the studio.

"Rockin' and jockin' with Rick Rakin, folks. Good music, good guests; it's going to be a goooood night." Rick's smooth voice filled Spence's headphones. "My guest this evening is Spence Collins. He's opening up Not Fade Away, the brand-new old vinyl store in downtown Milwaukie…Oregon that is. Love me some vinyl, yes, I do. The music won't fade away with Spence Collins to keep it alive."

"Thank you, Rick," Spence said, his delivery sounding like a car commercial. *Pull back.* "We're pretty excited about the store. And we're jazzed about the event we're holding for it. No pun intended."

"Jazz event, folks. And I'm not going to give away any spoilers, but you've got an outstanding lineup of the best of the best in town, Spence. I know your knowledge of music is pretty wide. We can sit here all day and go from bluegrass to grunge, but since we're a jazz station, let's stick to the cooooool old stuff."

"Depends on your definition of old, but okay, fire away." Spence leaned into the boom of the microphone, hoping he wasn't too close and popping his *P*s. He smiled to himself, remembering his conversation with Jess, the immortal member of the Gaines household in Richmond. Jess had seen all the greats over his 141 years. This was nothing compared to that experience. He relaxed. *Just like sitting in*

Monroe Park, talking with Jess Gaines.

"How many albums do you have in your personal collection, Spence?"

"I'd say about five or six thousand. But don't ask my wife, Jean. She'd say there were twenty thousand, given how many times we've moved them from state to state. Those suckers are heavy. As for the store, my business partner, Bill Flannery, and I have purchased massive collections over the past year. Baby boomer downsizing is our upsizing. I'd say we're opening the store with a good twenty to thirty thousand albums."

"Hey, calling all you boomers out there. If you're sellin', Spence Collins is buyin'. What was the first album you ever bought?" Rick fingered his goatee. A practiced question.

"I still have that first album in my collection: Herb Alpert and the Tijuana Brass's *Whipped Cream & Other Delights* from 1965."

"Do you have a favorite artist or album?"

"Oh God, Rick, don't do that to me." Spence raised his dark-lashed brown eyes to the stained acoustic ceiling tiles and ran his fingers through his peppered gray hair. "I think it has to be the Rolling Stones, or maybe the Kinks. I can't get enough of B. B. King and Muddy Waters, though. The Stones' music emerged from the blues."

"Uh-huh, so right. What about vinyl rings your chimes?"

"The quality of the sound and the ability to interact with it. Putting the needle on an album is special. The snap and pop adds character and sucks you into the history. CDs and digital downloads sound fine, but they wipe away the patina. So sterile. It's like taking the crackly finish off a Chippendale desk and buffing out all the scratches and dings of history. The value is gone. Scars are part of life. Vinyl records age with you, but without Botox and plastic surgery."

"Yeah, my friend. Now you're talkin'. The cover art is good too," Rick added. "And nothing like the smell inside old album covers."

"You found my Achilles' heel, Rick. The woody aroma of age makes a great album cover even better. I'm a huge Rick Griffin fan. He did great posters, but he also created the art on the cover of Quicksilver's first album. It stands alone as one of the best, but when combined with the music, that album was magic. I had the privilege of meeting the artist before he died in a motorcycle accident in 1991. Nice guy. Quite a loss."

"Let's take our first caller." Rick pushed a button that was glowing red. "You're on the air with Spence Collins. What's your question?"

"Wasn't Okeh Records the first to put out the blues?" the caller asked. "Oh, and what's your favorite quote?"

"Good question. Are you stumped, Spence?" Rick bobbed his head, as if a few of his own favorite quotes popped into his head.

Spence knew his answer but let a moment of dead air hang to make the caller feel good. "Hmmm…Black Swan was the first, I believe. First one owned and managed by African Americans too. Launched the career of Ethel Waters. My favorite quotes are from Fats Waller. He had a lot of them, but he used to call the scotch he drank for breakfast 'liquid ham and eggs.'" Rick laughed out loud and so did Spence.

"Next caller. You're on the air."

"Hi, Rick. First-time caller. Spence, what do you see as the greatest musical feat?"

"Besides Bruce Springsteen playing for over four hours straight? That would have to be Louis Armstrong—fifty high Cs in a row."

"Next caller…What you got?" Rick's voice increased in animation.

"Do you have anything on Okeh Records, Spence?" the caller asked.

"I've got an old Lois Armstrong that was on Okeh. Given to me by the legendary Legs Flanders. I don't think I could ever sell it. Louis' first scat was on "Heebie Jeebies", recorded in Chicago in 1926."

"Legs Flanders...now there's a legend for you. We could do a whole program on him. Line three, you're on the air." Rick took a swig of coffee from of his KRIFF mug.

"How'd it all start, Spence? Jazz, I mean. I know the answer, but why don't *you* hit *me* with all you got."

Spence raised his brown eyes in surprise. He knew this voice. He had sat on a bench in Monroe Park in Richmond and listened to this ethereal voice: *Jess Gaines.*

"Uh...started with Buddy Bolden—king of New Orleans jazz. Doesn't get any better or bolder, or should I say Bolden?" Spence winced. Impressing the immortal Jess made him nervous. Nobody else had personally experienced so many decades of greats. "He played everything in a jazz way."

"Right on the money," the caller said. "Bix Beiderbecke, from Iowa, was a legend. Back in the twenties, was. Genius and tragedy. Prodigy at eight, but couldn't get it straight. No, sir. "Tiger Rag"—Dixieland Jazz Band—changed his life. He was a man of Louis Armstrong."

"Didn't he join the Wolverines band? Back in 1924?" Spence asked, trying to keep up.

"Had an unusual fingering style, yes he did. Made it sound clear and bright. That horn talked to me...ooooweeee. Quite a shame to lose him at 'jus twenty-eight from the witchy juice."

"You were there, caller?" Rick gawked at Spence in shock.

"I was. Yes I was."

"You don't sound that old. Who are you?" Rick now was more interested in the caller than the interviewee.

"Rather not say."

Spence opened and closed his mouth. *Be cool. Act like he's just another caller.* Rubbing his hands on the knees of his jeans to keep them from shaking, Spence leaned into the microphone. *Change the subject.*

"That Big Four beat...start of real jazz."

"So right, Mr. Spence." Jess's voice boomed through the

speakers. It sounded like it was coming from every corner of the studio. "Jelly Roll Morton brought the horn and clarinet together with three different tunes."

"Yeah, the beat. Always the beat," Rick added, nodding as if the three of them were bantering in a bar. "This caller sounds like he knows what he's talking about. I think you've met your match, Spence."

"This caller knows a helluva lot more than me," Spence said, humbled by Jess's words.

"If you can't keep the beat, they throw you outta the band." The caller's voice faded to nothing.

Spence closed his eyes and grazed his finger across one of the illuminated buttons on the console. *The music. Feet going every which way. Hands grabbing at anything. The horns...the piano. Magic. Jess.* "You are so right," Spence said, his voice shaky. "You should be sitting in this seat."

"Do you know this caller? Sounds like you do." Rick stared at Spence with a reverent expression.

"Yeah, you wouldn't believe how special this man is."

"Caller? Who are you?" Rick inquired, an urgency creeping into his voice. The sound system went silent. Spence went silent. Rick went silent.

Rick flinched when he realized how much dead air had passed. "Thank you, caller...whoever you are." He pushed the button, and the light went dark.

Spence waved his hand in a circle for Rick to ask him something, anything to keep the conversation going.

"So, Spence, we're almost out of time," Rick recovered. "Tell us about the event for the opening of Not Fade Away."

"Yes...right. On June 19th, we'll be holding a free concert in downtown Milwaukie. We'll be hosting the best jazz musicians in Portland and might have a few surprises too. No promises, but I'm trying to get the great Legs Flanders here for the event. My wife and I had the privilege of meeting him a few months ago. Stay tuned. If he comes, it'll be huge."

"You think Legs will really come out to Portland?" Rick sat up straight.

"We've got our fingers crossed."

"Well, whether he shows up or not, the event will be a summer highlight for jazz lovers." Rick pulled out a notepad and made several scribbles. "I think we'd better set up a live broadcast at the event. What do you say, Spence?"

"Deal!"

"I know Legs played with Louis Armstrong and Muddy Waters, but didn't he play with Ella Fitzgerald?"

"Oh, yeah. And Legs is a dear man. He's eighty-two now but spry as all get out. And, yes, he's every bit of seven feet tall. He salted my collection of jazz in the store with the best: Miles Davis, Dave Brubeck, Herb Ellis, the list goes on. I hope he can make it."

"We do too. We'll be there live, folks, recording every historic moment of the event. A first for Milwaukie—and if Legs shows up and plays, there'll be a traffic jam on McLoughlin Avenue. Stay tuned to KRIFF for all the updates."

"Thanks, Rick, for having me on the show." Spence felt like spinning a three sixty in his chair.

"Well, there you have it, KRIFF fans. If you want to be a part of history, then show up for the live event on the site of the Milwaukie Farmer's Market at McLoughlin and Harrison on Saturday, June nineteenth, eleven o'clock to three. Thank you to this week's riffin' guest, Spence Collins."

Jean stared at the speaker. Mycroft stared at the speaker because she was. *The immortal Jess talked to Spence on the radio—in public.*

The phone rang in the kitchen, jolting her out of her frozen state. She dashed to pick it up.

"I heard the show," Dillon said. "I can't wait for the concert!"

Only she and Spence knew how profound that statement was

from Dillon. Having had his hearing returned by Doc just three months ago, Dillon appreciated many things that most people took for granted.

"I'm so proud of him, sweetie. He was wonderful." The phone beeped, signaling another call. "I think Spence is calling in on the other line. Come over when you can."

"I will. And Jean?" Dillon paused. "He talked with Jess."

"Yes, he did."

"Love you."

"Love you too," she said, signing off and hitting the flash button. "Hi, honey! You were great, but—"

"Jean! It's Jon Segert. Want to go to Dromov's sentencing tomorrow? I think it's going to be a doozy. By the way, yes, Spence was great on the radio."

CHAPTER 3

Dromov Drops

On Monday afternoon, Jean dug her fingernails into Spence's knee with her eyes fixed on the empty jury box.

"Ow…quit it," Spence whispered through gritted teeth. He pried Jean's fingers from his black slacks.

Jean stared a hole in the back of Anthony Dromov's head when he leaned in to whisper to his team of lawyers. Even the man's coal-black hair looked smug. Hating Dromov wasn't enough; she wanted him to fry like an egg on a Houston sidewalk in August. Dromov's Ponzi scheme had threatened her and Spence's inheritance from Mary Coulter, as well as the savings of a number of his elderly clients. One of them was Legs Flanders.

The way Dromov had been caught was more than satisfying. Horus, the immortal hawk Jean and Spence had come to know and appreciate when they were first learning about the fabric, emerged from the talon during Jon Segert's interrogation of Dromov. The transformation terrified the man into confessing. Horus bit Dromov on the arm, which, Jean and Spence wondered, might still deliver repercussions. Leaving behind evidence of the wound only invited Agent Brick to add more notes to Jean's and Spence's files at the FBI. Special Agent Dan Brick had made it a personal mission to corner them about the fabric, the hawk, and their relation to Raleigh Coulter's death in London. No way were they going to tell him the truth, and neither was Jon Segert.

"How much longer are they going to be in there? This is torture." Jean's gaze shifted from Dromov to the door behind the jury box. This moment was the culmination of all they'd gone through with their painting, *The Dancing Boy*: the realization that their inheritance had nearly evaporated; facing Dromov in the interrogation with Horus; and watching Dillon Davis cry his eyes out at the death of his teacher. All because of greed. Dillon Davis had never been exposed to such sinister motivations. His only motivation was art.

"You know, Jean, a lot of good came out this," Spence said in a quiet voice. He had a sly smile on his face, as if he'd been reading her thoughts.

Spence was right. Good had come out of the ordeal. They'd been fortunate to get their money back because of Jon Segert's brilliant plan at the FBI. He'd used their valuable painting—their magical painting—to trap Dromov. Dillon's expert copy had helped to bring him down. The experience of meeting Legs Flanders, when they delivered his stolen money, could never be replicated. Also as a result, their relationship with Dillon had blossomed to the status of family member. And Jon had arranged for Dillon's incredible future position with the Art Crime Team at the FBI.

Jon Segert, sitting on the other side of Jean from Spence, was more than an agent; he was their dear friend who shared the secret knowledge of the magic. Jean and Spence had given the original painting—a Hendrick ter Brugghen with added strokes from Caravaggio's brush—to the FBI to sell to help restore the accounts of Dromov's victims. They'd done well.

Jon tapped Jean on the shoulder and pointed to the door by the podium. She locked on his bright blue eyes, twinkling with anticipation. The crow's feet around them deepened as the door squeaked open. The judge stepped into the courtroom and took his seat on the bench. Hushed mutters escalated as if giant termites chewed the wood wainscoting on the walls.

"Ladies and gentlemen, order please!" the judge announced, banging the gavel for emphasis. The door to the jury room squeaked open. The jurors streamed in, stone faced and appearing exhausted, as if they just wanted to go home, grab the remote control, and stare at an infomercial for Ginsu knives. The foreman handed the bailiff a piece of paper, longer than Jean anticipated.

The bailiff delivered it to the judge, who studied the words. From his expression and flushed skin, a tyrannical speech might be forthcoming.

"Anthony Dromov, will you please stand and face the court?" The tension of formality tightened the air in the courtroom. Jean squeezed Spence's hand, and like hers, it was sweaty.

Dromov stood, holding his right arm and making a show of his injury. No doubt he expected to be fully vindicated. His lawyers rose, stiff legged, whispering to each other. Jean moved to stand too, but Spence pulled her back. She plopped down on the wooden bench.

"Mr. Dromov…this court listened to your testimony, and also to that of all witnesses for both sides. The jury has rendered their conclusion." A screech emanated from the flexible neck of the microphone as the judge pulled it forward. Not so flexible. He leaned in and read the charges without raising his eyes.

"Anthony Dromov, you are here found guilty on all charges: securities fraud, investment advisor fraud, mail fraud, wire fraud, international money laundering to conceal and disguise the proceeds of specified unlawful activity, perjury, false statements, and finally, making a false filing with the Securities and Exchange Commission. The total penalty is a maximum of 145 years in prison and a fine of $12,260,000, plus restitution."

The judge took off his glasses and tossed them on the podium, rubbing his tired eyes with his thumb and forefinger.

"Mr. Dromov, I must say, in all my years, I have never tried a case as heinous as this," he said, his eyes still closed. "You not only squandered the life savings of numerous victims—some too elderly to even appear in this court—but you made a mockery of your profession and of mine." He paused with the wood gavel in his hand and bored his gaze into Dromov. "This court is adjourned."

Bang!

The judge descended the steps. His black robe disappeared with only a split second to spare before it would have jammed in the door.

Jean hugged Spence and then Jon. Spence shook Jon's hand. Jean blew out a breath as Dromov was cuffed and escorted out of the court, shouting his innocence the entire way.

Nash Winthrop, released on a technicality for supplying insider tips to Raleigh Coulter and Dromov, slipped out the back door of the courtroom. Jean happened to catch sight of him before he disappeared but didn't say anything. She wasn't interested in bringing down the mood.

"You know, guys, this case wouldn't have come this far without your help," Jon said as he, Jean and Spence emerged into the courthouse's marble lobby.

"And Horus's too. We can't forget him," Spence added. "How much did you find in those off-shore accounts?"

"About seventy million—give or take. Traced the cash through his bogus name: Arthur Williams. Now we can start liquidating the hard assets to get these people their money. There's an equal amount Dromov put into art. The Vermeer alone is a good chunk of it."

"What's going to happen to *The Dancing Boy*?"

"We'll talk about that one. Gerrod Barnes wants to buy the painting at top dollar."

"But—" Jean did not like the idea of that man, a shifty antiques dealer in London who only just barely managed to stay within the law, owning the painting.

"Jean…don't start with me." But Jon was smiling.

Jean smiled too. "Let's celebrate."

Jon's gaze was distracted by something just behind Jean. He took his hands from his pockets and ran one of them over his sandy blond crew cut. "Don't look now. Your favorite FBI agent is coming over to us."

Agent Dan Brick sauntered up to the trio with a smug expression on his face. Jean kept hers deadpan. His immovable dark hair and stony face signaled his readiness to instigate a fight. His square jaw was tight.

"Brick," Spence said, half-hearted, and passed on shaking the agent's hand.

"Mr. Collins. Mrs. Collins." Brick's patronizing voice got under Jean's skin. "Have you given any more thought regarding our conversation about that fabric?" Dan shifted his squinty gaze from Spence to her and then settled on Jon with a self-satisfied smirk.

"Lighten up, Dan," Jon warned. "We wouldn't be here right now watching Dromov go behind bars if not for these two."

"Nothing to talk about." Jean glared at Brick. "You seem to have it all figured out. Actually, I think you're itching to make more notes in our file."

"I'm gathering quite a collection of fascinating notes in your file, Mrs. Collins. That fabric is evidence in an unsolved murder where the facts don't quite add up. And the statements you and Mr. Collins made don't add up either."

Jean glanced at Spence and then to Jon. She remained silent.

"What? A hawk got your tongue, Mrs. Collins?" Brick threw her an unyielding stare. "I'm going to get that fabric back from Cairo and see it for myself."

"You'll do no such thing, Brick."

"Try me."

On Monday evening, Spence came through the front door with a stack of mail. He tossed the pile on the kitchen island and stepped to the open dining area. Solace resided behind the door of the teak credenza: his humidor. Normally a Friday night ritual, he trumped the schedule by plucking a Cohiba Cuban cigar from the collection and running the length of it under his appreciative nose.

"I'm sitting out on the patio," he said, still seething from their run-in with Dan Brick. The man's snark embedded in his skin like a chigger.

Jean kept her eye on him, sure if she mentioned anything about the exchange at the courthouse she'd only be chumming the waters. She, too, smarted from the FBI agent's words. Jon Segert had stormed off when Brick ruined their celebratory moment.

Two glasses of wine were already poured and breathing on the kitchen island. Jean tucked the stack of mail under her arm and carried the two glasses outside. A small private patio with sliding doors off the dining room offered a quiet place to relax among hanging baskets of bleeding hearts.

"Here. Calm down." Jean set a glass of Velvet Devil merlot in front of him. She scooted out one of the lounge chairs, sat, and inhaled the deep pine scent of the soaring fir trees surrounding their property. She followed the path of an enormous predatory bird overhead. An osprey flew into one of the treetops with a screaming mouse, probably a rat.

"I wish that bird had Brick in his talons," Spence said, puffing to light his cigar. "I'd let it eat the sucker alive."

Jean blew out a breath but didn't otherwise respond. In the tight pause, she flipped through the stack of mail, reciting the senders as she tossed the envelopes on the glass table.

"Defenders of Wildlife, Doctors without Borders, AARP, Humane Society, the New for the Wall fund-raiser for the museum, the final contract from the festival caterers—" A white number ten envelope softened her insides. She held it up and flicked the corner. "Well, Mr. Grumpy Head, this ought to make you feel better."

Spence set the cigar in the ashtray and leaned in for a closer view. The return address said *Legs Flanders*, nothing else. He raised his gaze and smiled.

"You think?"

"Open it and see. This could be your moment." Jean sipped her wine and studied his face.

Spence slipped on his glasses and tore the flap. He pulled out the lined sheet of paper ripped from a spiral-bound notebook. Before he started to read, he took one more puff, savoring the moment.

She waited, hoping Spence wasn't going to be disappointed.

"What did he say?" Jean jiggled her knee and tried to interpret the expression on Spence's face. She knew he was purposely trying to make it void of emotion, just to play with her. Which probably meant good news. Legs's whispering voice filled her head from the afternoon they'd spent with him in Washington, DC. *Please say you're coming, Legs,* she replied silently now.

Spence raised his deep-brown eyes, a whole world swimming inside them.

"Well, Miss Crazy Eyes...he's coming. He still has your kiss. What were you two doing when I took his records out to the car?"

"No way. He said that?"

"Way." Spence handed her the note.

Dear Spence,

Thank you for writing. Maybe I do got one good gig left in me. I need to come to you 'cause you got my harp. How else can I blow? I'm bringing Wheezy. He's my piano man. Hope that's keeping with your hospitality. Be in Portland on June seventeenth. Can you fetch us at the airport? Flight 472 at 3:15 p.m. We got our tickets. Guess me and Wheezy back on the road. Tell Miss Crazy Eyes I got her kiss in my hutch.

Legs

Jean raised her eyes. "Wheezy?"

"Better call the piano store and rent the Steinway they have in the window," Spence suggested, sitting back and rocking in the lounge chair.

"And you'd better rent an RV. We'll need a place for them to rest away from the heat during the festival. If Wheezy's seven feet tall like Legs, then neither of them will fit in the guest room bed. I'll change the sheets just in case. Maybe we should set them up in a hotel."

"I don't think so. They'll want to stay with us. Plus, it'll be easier to get them around if they stay here. I'll be at the store with Bill, setting up the last of the inventory. Come get me on the way to the airport."

"Oh, Lord. I need to start another list."

CHAPTER 4

Egypt Can You Hear Me?

At six o'clock on Tuesday morning, Dan Brick arrived at the empty FBI offices and closed his door. He checked his watch. The ten-hour time difference between Portland and Cairo forced an early start to his day. At least the office was quiet. He stepped behind his desk, clean and polished with only a phone, blotter, his computer, and a subpoena centered in front of him. The credenza was void of anything. He wanted only facts on his desk.

The Dromov case had created quite a win for Jon Segert. But Jon wasn't so successful on the Raleigh Coulter case. If Dan could swoop in and clean up the mess, a trifecta of points would come his way: solve an unsolved case, put Jon in his place, and reveal the cover-up connection with Jean and Spence Collins. Those two were up to something.

The investigation into Raleigh Coulter's death in London had become an obsession. Placing the blame on a giant hawk was too easy. But something unexplainable took place, according to Jon. The key to solving what happened inside Raleigh's taxi lay with Jean and Spencer Collins. They knew more than they'd offered in their interview, and Jon Segert had supported the smoke screen. Jon's loyalties needed realignment.

A yellow sticky note, tucked under the padded edge of his blotter, held the answer to solving this case. He plucked out the folded paper and stared at the phone number for Anhur Kumar, the executive director of the Cairo Museum. The subpoena he'd acquired ensured Kumar's cooperation. He'd go to Egypt himself to get his hands on the thing, if necessary. Dan rehearsed his official words to get the fabric back to the United States as he called the number.

On the third ring, the line connected. Dan flicked the corner of the subpoena as Kumar identified himself. The Egyptian accent bathed his smooth voice in professional formality.

"Yes, my name is Special Agent Dan Brick of the FBI in Portland, Oregon." Dan let the words sink in. "A piece of physical evidence in a murder case is currently on display in your museum. I'd appreciate your cooperation to return it."

A moment of silence lingered over the Atlantic Ocean, the wheat fields of Kansas, and the Cascade Mountains. The quiet air crawled over Mount Hood before settling in the FBI offices.

"I believe you are mistaken, Agent Brick." Kumar's voice took on an immediate wariness, signaling he was well aware of what evidence was being referred to.

Careful with this man. He clearly has a way of making people feel stupid. "Fabric," Brick said, emphasizing the F. "A piece of fabric was taken from the scene of the alleged homicide of Raleigh Coulter, an American investment manager, in London back in September of last year. The case remains unsolved and that artifact is important to getting to the bottom of what happened."

"We house thousands of Egyptian relics in this museum, many of which are encased in fabric. I can assure you, nothing in this institution can help you in your investigation."

"Please don't insult me, Mr. Kumar. You know, very well, what fabric—the one with three birds. It was a recent donation to your museum by Jean and Spencer Collins and needs to be brought back to the United States immediately."

"I'm sorry...not possible. The Nefertari piece is much too important and valuable. Any discussion about it being taken out of Egypt will not be considered."

"I have a subpoena. There doesn't need to be a discussion, a negotiation, or even an argument," Dan declared. "The only thing left to discuss is how we're going to transport the piece back to Oregon. And needless to say, I'd expect this to stay between us. Please don't call the Collinses. They may be implicated in the crime."

"But their donation—"

"No. They're not to know when, where, or how it gets here."

"Send me a copy of this subpoena. A meeting with my board must be called to discuss the request. I will need some time—through the end of the week at a minimum. May I give you a return call with their decision by Friday afternoon?"

"No decision to be made, Mr. Kumar. Don't waste my time. I'll come to Egypt. We'll gather the damned thing up, stuff it in a bag, and get on a plane with it. This isn't hard. What's the big deal?"

"Agent Brick…this is, as you say, a very 'big deal.'"

Anhur Kumar's gaze fixed on the handset of his desk phone after he hung up from the call. He ran his hand through his closely cropped dark hair and smoothed the sides into place. He loosened the knot on his red-striped tie and released the top button of his starched white shirt. His pulse pounded against the cloth. *Calm down. Think.*

Agent Brick had no idea of the fabric's power. If he did, he would not have been so cavalier in his attitude. Anhur recalled the events he himself witnessed and recorded. Only three people knew of that miraculous transformation: Jean, Spencer, and him. *Secrets.*

The French doors leading to the balcony of his office drew his gaze. The phoenixes had sat on the railing outside on that warm afternoon after the Collinses had released them. The last soul the phoenixes took into immortality was an elderly woman named Mary Coulter. *Where was she now?* With the assault of noise outside, Anhur was suddenly overcome with embarrassment for the modern human race. Angry chants from the gathered crowd of protesters in the square below offered only sharp reality to the serene memory.

The air beside him rippled. A rush of heat brushed his face as he stared in fascination. He wasn't alone.

Anhur's eyes widened as the form took shape and clarified. A woman of about sixty-five stood before him, her hazel gaze inquisitive and tender. Her style of tan tweed jacket and skirt appeared to be classic and timeless. A curious glow outlined her visage. She gave him a sad smile, one that hinted of loneliness.

"Take the fabric back to Portland, Mr. Kumar." This specter had a voice, lyrical and smooth.

"Who are you?" Anhur reached out and offered her his hand, eager to touch immortality. Warm. Soft. Her hazy outline left him transfixed.

"I haven't given you proper thanks for helping Jean and Spence get home to transform me last year. As you can see, they arrived in time."

"Mary Coulter?" Anhur's mouth went dry. A gallon of water couldn't quench his thirst.

"Yes. I wouldn't be standing here now without your help." Mary's warm smile turned cool. "You have a decision to make. Not an easy one, I'm afraid, but considering the growing hostility in Tahrir Square below, the choices are few."

"How can I keep the phoenixes safe? Not here. Not there."

"Mr. Kumar, the fabric is more than an artifact. You can't deny its power by hiding the phoenixes in a vault. They live and breathe, as I do, and make decisions based on worthiness. You can only care for this heirloom of the ages, not control its fate."

"Indeed. I cannot." Anhur bowed his head, relenting to Mary's words.

"I believe you're obligated to take the fabric back to Portland. Others will care too, as you do, if they're given the opportunity."

"Trust is a difficult emotion to embrace for such a precious object."

"People are the concern, Mr. Kumar, not the fabric. The birds know how to protect themselves."

"But—" Anhur stopped. Mary Coulter evaporated. He held out his hand and swirled the wisps of her that remained. *She lives.*

Anhur turned back to the glass of the door, contemplating the request. His mirrored reflection told him this was a fortuitous development. His dark eyes burned with the image of Mary Coulter, eclipsing the one of senseless violence.

"Out of chaos is born opportunity," he whispered.

The recent political unrest in Cairo racked him with worry over the fabric's safety. Only last week, protesters had stormed the museum's main floor, destroying several precious and irreplaceable artifacts. In their blind fury, the hoodlums smashed two cases and defaced their resting royal mummies. Thieves. Thugs. Art had never escaped the grip of politics through the ages. What did politics have to do with priceless antiquities? To destroy one's relics of history was to sabotage a foundation of lessons for humanity's future course. A repeat of history. No different from the ancient tombs being plundered by greed and politics within years of being sealed. But what made so many priceless pieces so valuable and important was their tangible reflection of culture, politics, and strife. For thousands of years the rise and fall of regimes were marked in art. A full circle. A conundrum. Treasures had been stolen over the centuries and, like the Nefertari fabric, found their way back to the light. Jean and Spencer Collins had played a valuable role in not only returning the relic to Egypt but in confirming what he believed of its power of transformation. But this kind of politics, the one turning dangerous in the streets outside in the square, had nothing to do with the museum. The vandals had acted out of anger, frustration, and repression. This unrest, too, would eventually be told through art.

After this latest incident, Anhur had ordered the case with the sacred fabric removed from public display and stored in a locked vault in the museum's basement. Taking it out of the country may, very well, be an opportunity to ensure its safety—for history's sake. Mary's words filled him as if they had come from everywhere. *You can't hide it away in a vault.*

The dial on his office safe in the bookcase gleamed in the sunlight, drawing his attention. Anhur ran his hand over the spines of reference books flanking the steel case: Valley of the Kings on one side, Valley of the Queens on the other. He spun the sequence of numbers. As if a small, modern tomb, the safe held an envelope in a hidden recess. The flash drive. He slipped it in the pocket of his suit jacket.

Anhur locked his office door and moved with quick, determined steps toward the elevator. Inserting his security card, he pressed *B* and descended to the basement.

History lingered in the vast storage area. Sealed tombs of treasures. More artifacts were housed in the vaults than were on display in the public spaces. Over the past month, Anhur had systematically removed several of the most important relics: ancient gold jewelry, stone hieroglyphs, weapons of the gods…and the precious Nefertari fabric.

A small key unlocked vault 2-36. Anhur stepped inside and flipped on the light. A shimmer of vivid colors greeted him from behind the Plexiglas case mounted on a rolling pedestal. The case had been designed to be a singular display in the center of the exhibition hall, allowing visitors to view the fabric from all sides. But the phoenixes only breathed life for him—the enlightened, the knowledgeable.

"Hello, my lovely ones." Anhur set his hands on the thick Plexiglas.

The three phoenixes in the fabric turned their heads in sequence toward their protector, studying him with curiosity in their eyes. They seemed to know he was not just paying a visit. Their red-crowned heads threw off an ethereal neon glow in the halogen light. The snaking green vines with tiny white flowers seemed to shimmer and move. For Anhur, they were a garden of possibility. The knot in his stomach tightened. No other option existed but to remove them from Egypt while the situation remained unsettled.

"We're moving you to the United States," he whispered. "We

must protect you from harm, from theft, from the world as it is."

The phoenixes blinked. Pure. Aware.

"Do you want to fly again…with me?"

Anhur stared at the phoenixes for a moment. The case warmed beneath his hand. He lifted his fingers away from the Plexiglas, turned, and shut off the light. He re-locked the door as the transport arrangements whirled through his mind. To tell the truth to this FBI agent carried risk, but a risk he was willing to take to keep the artifact safe. He had a long thirteen-hour flight to decide, a private flight he needed to convince Agent Brick that he would make alone.

Time to call a meeting of the board.

CHAPTER 5

The Long and Short Invasion

The day of Legs and Wheezy's arrival was a whirlwind of activity as the final preparations came together for the jazz festival and the opening of Not Fade Away. Once their plane landed, tending to Legs and Wheezy's needs would leave Jean and Spence little time for anything else.

Spence set up the last of the inventory at the store as Bill trailed behind him with a pricing gun. The bins were separated into rows: jazz, blues, swing, rock (classic and modern), and country. At the front wall by the entrance, they had created a small section of tiki lounge music, one entire collection acquired from a passionate lover of all things Hawaiian, particularly Don Ho. The collector liquidated the records in favor of acquiring vintage Hawaiian shirts. On Jean's request, Spence relented to a small section of Broadway cast albums. All agreed that classical was more than covered by their competitor, Music Millennium, in downtown Portland.

Spence positioned the poster for the jazz festival and taped the corners to the front window. His stomach jumped when Jean pulled to the curb in the T-Bird and waved.

"I gotta go, big guy. Jean and I need to pick up Legs and Wheezy at the airport. I think we've done everything we can do. You finish pricing, and I'll bring us two legends."

"Better get your butt moving," Bill warned, "and make sure we have good audio on Saturday. The equipment we talked about should be top-of-the-line and really loud."

"Jean's got all that arranged with the event management company."

"And Rick Rakin has the soundboard all worked out for the live broadcast?"

"Yep. And we'll have CDs to sell here at the store."

"And the lighting? Blue and gold gels, right?"

"Jean's got that covered too. Scares the hell out of me, though. I have to trust she knows her stuff. Broadway's not that much different from a concert, but whatever she's doing it'll be big."

"The piano is lined up for Wheezy?"

"Shiny black Steinway. Jean did a deal to rent it for the day."

"Cool." Bill bobbed his head with relief. "We need a really tall stool for Legs. I have one at home in my basement. I'll bring it on Saturday."

With his hand on the door handle, Spence gawked at Bill. "Was that our pre-concert staff meeting? We're two days out."

"Yeah. I think we're ready."

Bill and Spence pointed to each other from across the store. In unison, they shouted, "Thank God for Jean!"

Jean and Spence stood in the waiting area as passengers exited the terminal. Bright sunlight flashed through the overhead windows of the atrium design. Jean shaded her eyes to get a better view. She had no idea how to spot Wheezy. At least she'd be able to see Legs above the crowd; he'd be hard to miss.

"The flight landed. Where are they?" Jean pressed

"Relax. They can't get by us. Maybe they're wandering around the gate area, thinking we can go inside to meet them. They don't travel much anymore."

"What if they can't find the exit? Should I ask someone from TSA to search for them?" Jean wanted to push through the stream of passengers coming at her. She pictured two elderly men wandering the terminal in an endless circle until they dropped.

"Here they come, honey—there's Legs." Spence pointed to the new group of exiting flyers; a dark, shiny bald head towered above all the others. The first of possible crises had been avoided.

"He looks just the same. Where's Wheezy?"

Legs lumbered toward them with a smooth gait. He appeared to be talking to himself. Then he stopped as another passenger took him aside. Jean could hear him laugh, deep and genuine with a touch of humility. Jean bobbed and weaved to catch a glimpse of what he was doing.

"Don't know. Didn't Wheezy come too?" Spence said. He, too, had a creeping concern, sharing her vision of a Steinway with no player.

Pulling a pen from his breast pocket, Legs signed the man's boarding pass and leaned down to hand it to someone else. A child? The passenger, though, beamed as he stared at the paper and shook Legs's hand.

"What's he doing?" Jean craned her neck.

"I think he's giving an autograph to someone. We'll find out soon enough. Here he comes."

A beaming smile of yellowed teeth greeted them as Legs resumed moving toward the exit. He spotted Jean and Spence and waved, his arm stretched like an extension rod above the crowd. The navy blue pinstripes on his white cotton shirt accentuated the span. Jean had an urge to check the label on the back of his Levis for their length, which must be upwards of fifty inches. Their eyes traveled downward; next to him, talking a mile a minute, was an elderly man who must be Wheezy. He resembled a Virginia ham in black wingtips and black-framed glasses as big as his head. The ham waved. Jean waved back. The wisp of a gray comb-over completed his distinctive visage.

As he moved closer, Jean figured Wheezy barely reached the five-foot mark. The thick lenses of his oversize glasses magnified his deep-blue eyes. As round as he was tall, Wheezy might have reached Legs's middle shirt button—if he jumped. Although elderly, roughly the same age as Legs, Wheezy had skin that looked soft and peachy, as if it had never seen sun.

"Well, hey, Music Man and Miss Crazy Eyes," Legs said and reached out to shake Spence's hand. Jean wrapped her arms around his middle. "Don't squeeze, now." He patted her back. "Can't talk when I gotta go. There a drain hole in this place? I could use it."

Jean laughed and pointed toward the restroom. Her gaze followed Legs's long strides, still fascinated by his height.

"I guess Legs isn't going to properly introduce me." The short man rolled his eyes. "He's had to go since we crossed over Idaho. I'm famous too, by the way." He clucked his tongue and pointed his finger in the shape of a gun. "Wheezy Beevers," he announced, sticking out his hand and wiggling his fingers. In contrast to the rest of him, he had curiously long ones. Spence stooped to give Wheezy's hand a vigorous shake.

Jean pressed her lips together. Spence smirked. The way he said his name was humorous on several levels. They hadn't known Wheezy's last name until he said it.

"Welcome to Portland!" Spence announced and threw up his hands. "We're so glad you and Legs came."

"Where's my hug?" Wheezy said and reached for Jean. "If you're dishing those out, how about laying one right here?" He opened his mouth in a soundless laugh like Joe E. Brown. His top dentures dropped a little.

As Jean gave Wheezy a squeeze, she thought he felt spongy like a marshmallow.

"Legs wouldn't stop talking about you both for five—count 'em—*five* hours." He held up his fingers and rolled them in a rhythmic wave. "I almost opened the emergency exit and threw him out, but I didn't want to be interrogated by the TSA. Who knows what's in my record." Wheezy gave them another windy Joe E. Brown laugh, scrunching his eyes. Jean now knew why his name was

Wheezy.

"Any friend of Legs is a friend of ours," she declared.

"Kind of you to pick us up, but I don't know how that gangly monster will fit in your car."

"We brought the T-Bird. Convertible."

"What year?" Wheezy peered over the frames of his glasses, suspicious. She figured if she said an uncool date, he'd refuse to be taken to the car.

"Ahhh...1963." She smirked.

"Color?"

"Chalafonte Blue...aqua...with white piping around the seats."

"Hot damn! I'll get in then." Wheezy clapped and rubbed his hands together.

"Not until Legs comes out of the restroom," Spence reminded.

"All right. We'll wait. Now I have to go. Prostate the size of a damned volleyball."

"You'd better hoof it if you want to catch up to Legs." Jean shook her finger at the men's restroom.

"Shoot. I'll be in and out before that piece of scaffolding is done." Wheezy handed Spence his satchel. "Hold this. Be careful; it's hot. My sheet music's in there. Tsssssss!"

Jean laughed as Wheezy waddled toward the restroom. She leaned toward Spence. "I think we're in for a run for our money."

He thumped the satchel. "No doubt. Tsssssss."

CHAPTER 6

Homecoming

"Sorry, guys. Only one guest room," Jean said as she unlocked the front door. "You'll need to bunk together. I hope that's not a problem."

"Pay no mind. All right by me," Legs said.

"Love the car, but the T-Bird messed up my 'do.'" Wheezy smoothed his wisp and pushed ahead as Legs ducked, trying not to smack the top of his head on the doorframe.

"This is one crazy-lookin' house." Legs's gaze made an arc around the triangle-shaped clerestory windows and multi-level, open design. "One 'pressive cat up there, yes, he is. Big as a bear. Scare me in the night, he will."

Mycroft stared at them with his ears sticking through the steel rail of the open upstairs hallway. He puffed his fur at the long and short invasion, trying to be intimidating.

"He ain't sleepin in my bed," Legs groused.

"Cork it, Goldilocks. We're sharing, remember?" With his hands on his hips, Wheezy's gaze rose to the second floor catwalk. "Stairs? Are you serious?"

Jean immediately had doubts about not arranging a local hotel for Legs and Wheezy. A selfish decision.

"I'll use Wheezy as a pillow and prop myself with that crazy cat," Legs said. "Can wedge that bear cub up under my knees. Jus' don't feed Wheez nothin' bad."

"I'll take the bags upstairs. You guys put your feet up. You've had a long trip." Spence glanced at her. He had doubts too.

"Nap time!" Wheezy announced. "How about Mexican for dinner? Not that *nouveau riche* Mexican, either. I want the high-test stuff with refried beans and guacamole."

"While you guys take a snooze, I'll go get the RV. You'll need a quiet place to hang out at the festival before your grand finale."

"Don't forget to stock the fridge."

"Water and snacks—check," Jean said. "I can steam up some tamales for dinner, Wheezy. They're all ready to go." Flipping a page on her notepad, she added several items to the grocery list.

"Perfect! Ta-ta-tamales! Sound good, Legs?"

"Lord help me." Legs shook his head.

Ahead of them, Mycroft trotted toward the guest bedroom and sat in the doorway. Jean laughed and did a scan of the downstairs. She wasn't sure whether Wiley might appear, and if he did, how she'd explain his presence. Worry about it later. The quiet break would allow her to go over the list of final arrangements for the concert.

Wheezy took one step at a time up the stairs as he grasped the rail. "C'mon cat. Taking a nap. No hogging."

The house was quiet when Spence came through the mudroom with two grocery bags. Jean clicked away on her laptop at the dining room table, turning with a finger to her lips.

"Shhh…"

"Still asleep?" he whispered.

She nodded. "Got the RV?"

"No problem. Two beds, a bathroom, and a kitchen. I stopped and loaded the fridge with snacks. Legs needs to duck, though. The inside is only six feet. I measured."

"Dillon's on his way over to join us for dinner. He wants to see Legs and meet Wheezy."

"You think they're okay up there?" Spence set the bags on the counter.

"Go up and take a peek. You won't believe the scene—or who's with them. Hilarious." Jean abandoned the computer to follow him.

The risers squeaked as Spence crept up the stairs to the guest room. He pushed open the door a few inches to peek inside. Both men were on their back sucking in air. A warm breeze circled the room through the screen of the open sliding glass door. Legs's bare feet hung over the bottom of the bed. Wheezy's black socks hit about half way. Mycroft had wedged himself between them like a fuzzy bratwurst in a bun, completing the trio of snores. Two pairs of shoes sat side-by-side on the floor next to the bed: size 13 Hush Puppies and a pair of size 6 black wingtips. Wiley lay on his back in front of the screen, illuminated black paws to the breeze.

"Priceless." Spence padded down the stairs and stopped on the landing. He turned to Jean. "How do we explain Wiley?"

"I doubt the guys are even aware of his presence. He might be gone when they wake up…but if they do meet him, we're going to have to tell the truth."

"They can handle it…I think."

CHAPTER 7

Life with a Different View

On Saturday morning, the FBI offices were teeming with staff, as if a normal work day. Jon needed a couple of hours before going down to Milwaukie for Jean and Spence's festival. Too much to do. Too many cases. The only one conspicuously absent was the chief. Jon sat in his office and reviewed the transactions of Jason "Kip" Forrester's bank accounts one more time. They smelled rotten. Kip was the final lead he's squeezed out of Nash Winthrop when Jon had interrogated him. The chief didn't believe he was closing in on this case, but Jon believed, without question, he could floss the BS from between the money lines.

He needed a breakthrough to prove his theory. Insider trading was like an iceberg: 10 percent stuck its peak above the water; the remainder lurked beneath in the depths of an ocean of public ignorance. Wall Street didn't play fair with the average investor in a dingy.

Each wire transfer, both incoming and outgoing, matched up with precision to the timing of press releases from four companies over the last six months. In every case, funds were wired out to make a stock purchase two weeks before the release of major news. Then, the same number of shares was sold three days after the public announcement—with gains of more than 300 percent. The source of the profit-taking ran the gambit: mergers, product releases, partnerships, and corporate takeovers. Kip had inside tips. Jon would bet

Forrester paid kickbacks from his profits to get them. But he needed proof.

"Jenny?" he called out.

His assistant appeared in the doorway with one eye narrowed and her lips pursed. She'd come to work in jeans, an oversize man's white cotton shirt, not ironed, and a cricket-green Scrunchie in her long brown hair. Not too far off from her normal work attire. "There's a little button on your phone labeled with my name. That's how civilized people call other people."

Jon smirked. He knew Jenny hated being summoned with a yell, but it was the only thing he could tease her with. She was the best damned assistant on the West Coast of the FBI. He'd be lost without her.

"Pull the file on Nash Winthrop. *Please.*"

"Haven't heard that name in a while. He was the barfer, right?"

"Yep. The guy who barfed."

"This ought to be fun. Be right back." Jenny disappeared as if a hook pulled her from the doorway.

Nash Winthrop had been Raleigh Coulter's college roommate. He'd slipped through Jon's fingers on a technicality. Turning off the camera to hide the talon's transformation extracted a confession and names, but the stunt didn't help to put Nash behind bars. And he deserved to be incarcerated. As the insider at VEY Steel, Nash sold both Coulter and Dromov information. In his case, though, feeding a tip about a pending merger had backfired. The transaction never happened, leaving Raleigh in serious debt and Nash out of a job. For Raleigh the desperation led to his pulling the stupid stunt of stealing the fabric from Jean, which ultimately led to his death. He was on his way to sell it to an antique dealer in London named Gerrod Barnes, the very man who later cooperated with the FBI to recover *The Dancing Boy* painting and corner Dromov. Now, Barnes wanted to buy the painting as part of the liquidation of Dromov's assets. Jon agreed with Jean that was far from ideal, but he knew they both wanted restitution for the victims of the fraud.

Jenny breezed into his office fanning the thick stack of pages in Nash's file. It landed with a *thunk* on Jon's desk.

"Go get 'em, tiger," she said and dashed back to her cubicle.

Jon tapped his pen on the folder. The situation might come full circle. Nash was still desperate and unemployed. He was acquainted with Forrester, probably selling tips to him. Nash would sell out his mother for a buck. *The Dancing Boy* painting over his credenza drew his gaze. Jon had insisted on keeping the masterpiece in his office for safety, but the truth was that he enjoyed the presence of the enchanted work. Doc's immortal words haunted him. *Follow the money, Mr. Segert. Follow the money.*

"You know how to solve this, don't you?" he said aloud, shaking his finger at the canvas. The angelic image of the young boy didn't move, remaining frozen in mid-step of his celebratory dance.

Jon checked the time. Now he was charged up to delve into this investigation, but he'd promised to stop by Spence's jazz festival. Legs Flanders and the Collinses, among Dromov's victims, might give him inspiration for making the next move. Plus, he was anxious to meet Legs in person.

He closed the files and plucked the talon from the center desk drawer. The thick, curved claw had become his security blanket, a partner, and a symbol of confidence. At some point he'd have to wean himself from Horus. The hawk was becoming an addiction. He dropped the talon in his pocket. Not yet.

Early that same Saturday morning, Nash Winthrop stepped through the door of his top-floor loft in the Pearl District, sweaty from a workout in the building's gym. His glass-lined sanctuary was hanging by a thread. The lifeline of extra income from tips to Coulter, Dromov, and Forrester had dried up. They'd all lost big money on the VEY Steel deal. But the fees had paid for Nash's custom furnishings and the endless view overlooking the Willamette River. A shaft of sunlight through the expanse of glass hit the cobalt-blue vase on the coffee table. The glint taunted him, a reminder of his last option: get back in step with Kip Forrester.

With his water bottle in hand, he leaned over the kitchen counter and perused the Arts & Entertainment section of the *Oregonian*. An article on a jazz concert in Milwaukie caught his eye when he read the headline, "Legs Flanders to Play Legendary Harmonica at Milwaukie Jazz Concert." He pored over the words to the end.

Legs was still alive? And playing with Wheezy Beevers too? Today? Nash glanced at the bills draining his savings that were piled inside the orange ceramic bowl meant for fruit. The harmonica, once owned by Muddy Waters, would be worth a fortune. The instrument might be a way to get into Kip's empire. With Raleigh Coulter dead and Tony Dromov in jail, Forrester stood between receiving a big check and having to serve lattes at Starbucks.

Kip collected famous instruments, and he'd certainly want this one. If Nash could get his hands on it, he'd not only make serious coin but possibly win a job out of the deal too. But the option to buy it outright wasn't a possibility with the current balance in his bank account.

Nash flashed on his interview with Segert. That talon. The memory of it moving and changing made his skin crawl. The stunt must have been done with some kind of new technology the FBI developed. He envisioned someone similar to Q, who provided cool toys to James Bond. Scared the hell out of him, though.

How stupid he'd been to react to the agent's questions. Giving Segert the actual names of his clients, especially Kip's name, had been a serious error in judgment. Kip mattered because Kip could give Nash a job. But it may not be an irreversible error. As far as Nash knew, Kip wasn't aware his name floated around Segert's FBI investigation. Nash needed to rectify the situation before Kip found out. Thank God the camera had been turned off or he, himself, would be in a cell right now, losing everything he'd worked so hard— too hard—for.

The orange bowl drew his gaze. He hadn't had the guts to open most of the envelopes inside it, but at least they were organized by due date. With a plan taking shape, Nash dropped the newspaper and the empty water bottle in the recycle bin. He had a couple of hours to hit the shower, get dressed, and head down to Milwaukie to fight for a parking space. Life would look different by cocktail hour.

CHAPTER 8

The Festival

Relief from the hot sun came in the form of puffy clouds floating over the crowd like a sunbrella. Families with strollers, elderly riders on scooters, and both the fit and the un-fit on bikes dotted the throngs of die-hard music fans. Some had only wandered in for a beer and a tamale or to check out what caused the traffic backup on McLoughlin Avenue.

With one more set to go before Legs and Wheezy, Jean peeked around the side of the stage and scanned the crowd. The numbers had grown exponentially since she'd checked an hour ago. A quick scan told her there were over four hundred milling about, waiting for the finale. The press releases she'd sent over the past two weeks had put the festival in the *Oregonian* and on the events calendars for more than eight senior living communities. Their brightly colored buses lined the side street. The chance to see Legs and Wheezy had drawn them away from swapping memories over a lively game of bingo.

Jon and Dillon stood near the taco truck, probably talking about Dillon's future career at the FBI. The milling crowd appeared to be having a good time. A group of fans had created a dance area in front, encroaching on the section set aside for those in wheelchairs. She waved at a hired security worker who, at the moment, wasn't securing anything. She'd have to keep an eye on that situation. Anticipation rippled through the audience as the Walking River Trio strolled on stage, a jazz combo of a drummer, pianist, and sax player. Spence had summoned the elderly players back into service from their retirement. He wanted them to play Dave Brubeck's "Take Five" to get the crowd ready for the big finish.

Jean's gaze settled on two forms with slight halos gravitating toward Jon. For her, they were hard to miss. She pulled on Spence's sleeve as he rushed by holding the necks of two beers in his hand, one for him and the other for Bill. She pointed and mouthed, *Doc and Jess.* A broad smile lit up his face.

"I hoped they'd come," he said. "They're here for the finale. We have fifteen minutes after Walking River."

Jean waved at Jon, who held up his beer in an air toast. At least the immortals wouldn't be alone.

The backstage area needed her attention. Everything had been inventoried for the grand close with Legs and Wheezy. The crowd noise cranked up a notch as the sax riff sailed over the lilting beat. The old guys still had it in them.

She adjusted the microphone on her headset.

"Dry ice in twelve minutes. Almost time for the finale." Her gaze shot across the stage to the other side. From behind the soundboard, Rick Rakin nodded his head. "You ready for the boys? Over."

"Am I ever. Over." Rick stuck up his thumb.

She spotted a lighting technician and trotted over to him. He gave her a tired sigh as he positioned the last spotlight on the rig.

"They're supposed to swivel up and down in alternate colors of gold and bright blue," she said, pointing to the light bar.

"Yeah. They'll go up and down. Don't worry." The guy's expression mocked her as if she had no idea what she was doing. Even the tattoo on his arm— a hissing panther—warned her to back off.

"But there aren't any color gels on these lights. I specifically ordered blue and gold ones." Jean kicked herself for not addressing this detail sooner.

"Nobody told me anything about colored gels."

"Please say you have some in the truck." Jean ran her hand

through her hair in frustration. "We need those colors for 'Got My Mojo Workin' with Legs and Wheezy"—she glanced at her watch— "in eleven minutes."

"I think I got some red ones somewhere."

"We can't use red! We're not shooting a porn film. Are you kidding?"

"Want me to get 'em or not?" The toothpick in his mouth churned in a practiced circle as he waited for her to answer.

"Get 'em." Jean glowered at the technician as he sauntered toward the stairs to his truck. "I'm not committing until you show them to me!" she shouted at his back. He didn't acknowledge her, and he probably wouldn't search too hard for the red gels either. Her gaze settled on Spence and Bill at the edge of the stage, bobbing their heads in time to the syncopated beat of the piano and swishing drum. Wrinkling her nose, she marched over to them.

She tapped Spence on the shoulder. "We have red gel lights for 'Mojo,' not blue and gold *like* I asked for."

"Red's cool. What do you think?" Spence smiled at Bill and took a pull from his microbrew.

"Boom-chicka-mow-mow!" Bill sang and rocked on his heels.

"You two are impossible. Spence, can you go get Legs and Wheezy? They're on after this band." Jean shook her head. "Oh— and Legs's harmonica?"

"Right here." Spence patted the right pocket of his jeans.

"Keep it together, buddy," Bill said. "You're going out to introduce them."

"Piece-a cake. Hold this." Spence handed Bill his beer and bolted to the metal steps at the far end of the backstage, jumping two at a time.

The lighting technician swaggered toward Jean. "I had one red, no others," he said.

"I want a credit!" she huffed. "Position the gel on the light directly over Legs."

"Whatever."

Jean stomped to the steps and waited at the threshold. Spence followed Legs, who pushed Wheezy from behind as he climbed to the backstage area. Wheezy rested on the top step to catch his breath. Jean held his arm.

"You okay, Wheezy?"

"Yeah, give me a minute. You put those damned things…there to torture me. Steps…are too high," Wheezy answered, gasping.

"What about you, Legs?"

"I'm fine. I'm fine."

When Legs entered the backstage, the technicians and roadies stopped rolling their cords. Their gazes rose and fixed on him.

"How y'all doin'?" Legs said, extending his long arm in a wave. Spence stood behind him and beamed.

Wheezy, having caught his breath, raised his hand too. He pointed at Legs with his thumb. "I make him look good."

The lilting rhythm of the swishing drum faded to nothing on "Take Five." The crowd's cheers drowned out the final cadence. As the band members took a bow and entered the backstage, they stopped in their tracks.

"Jesus, come take me! Legs Flanders?" The sax player raced to shake Legs's hand.

"Yes, he is." Wheezy grimaced and marched to the partition at the edge of the stage.

Jean rushed to his side. "I can't wait for you to play, Wheezy. The Steinway's ready." She threw Spence a worried glance. He caught her eye. She stepped over to him and whispered, "When you go out there, get the crowd whipped up for Wheezy. Give him five minutes to play by himself. I think his feelings are hurt. Legs is getting all the attention."

"Got it."

Jean hoped Spence didn't have too much beer in him to pull off an eloquent speech. But he never ceased to amaze her. She turned back to Wheezy.

"Spence wants you to play for a few minutes. The crowd will go crazy. You'll have the stage to yourself…all by yourself. They're waiting for you."

Wheezy patted her arm and wiggled his fingers. "These hands are magic, Jeany Weany. I have just the ticket."

She turned on her headset. "Spence is going on to introduce Wheezy." Jean blew Spence a kiss.

With combined excitement and confidence, Spence plucked the microphone from the stand.

"Thank you all for coming and for supporting Bill Flannery and me. Our vintage vinyl store is opening tomorrow. Not Fade Away has been our goal for many years. We're going to be the home of legends. And as we all know, legends never die. The one to play for you next has played with the greats, including the first lady of jazz, Ella Fitzgerald. This is an historic moment for me, the world of jazz, and you. It is my privilege to bring to you the amazing Wheeeeeezy Beevers!"

Wheezy stepped onstage with both hands over his head and his mouth open. He gave the crowd an exuberant smile. The two black dots of his wing-tip shoes carried him toward the piano bench. With a jump and a scoot, he stared at the keys. There was a moment of silence as everyone waited for a sound, any sound, to come from the Steinway.

Wheezy leaned into the microphone and skimmed his right hand down the full length of the keyboard, from the top C to the bottom. The audience erupted.

"In memory of my dear friend Fats Waller…'The Joint Is Jumpin'!'" His fingers sailed across the ivories as if they were coated in olive oil. The backstage went quiet as the roadies stopped to listen to Wheezy. Jean shut off her microphone. Her mouth popped open. Spence stood mesmerized. Bill set down his beer bottle. Linda held the edge of the stage at the front of the crowd, jumping up and down as if on a pogo stick. The joint jumped with her.

Stunned out of her trance at Wheezy's frenzied tickle of the top keys, Jean flipped the switch on her headpiece and shouted out instructions to the technicians.

"White lights, no red yet! Start the dry ice! Now! Go!" She turned to Spence. He had a blank look on his face. "The harmonica. Legs is ready. Are you?"

Spence inspected the carved letters on each end of the glinting metal. He handed her the instrument and floated to the edge of the stage to listen to Wheezy. Jean stepped to Legs's side and reached for his hands. She placed the harmonica in his palm. Desperate to feel his skill, she wrapped her fingers around his.

"They're waiting for you," she said.

Legs studied her face. His ebony eyes betrayed an expression Jean didn't recognize. A numbing vibration shot down her arms and transferred to Legs's hands. Tiny blue veins of electricity arced from the harmonica and raced around their entwined fingers.

"What you got goin' on there?" he said, tightening his squeeze.

"I don't know, I truly don't, but you're about to find out." Smoky trails of dry ice crept along the floor and engulfed their feet.

The crowd erupted as Wheezy pounded out the final riff and floated his hands away from the keys. He laughed out loud. Wheezy leaned into the microphone and said, "How about jumping with real Legs this time?"

Legs tilted his head to the stage. "That some kindness out there, what Spence did for old Wheez." He stared at their hands, still entwined. "You are somethin', really jumpin'."

"Not me...you. This joint hasn't even begun to jump yet." She tapped the harmonica. "This will only play for you, Legs." Jean turned and signaled for Spence to walk on stage.

With two long steps, Legs stood at the edge of the partition to shouts of his name. He nodded and gave her with a broad smile. The tightness in Jean's throat released a blur of tears in her eyes.

"Ladies and gents, what you've been waiting for!" Spence's voice echoed from the speakers. "Let me hear your mojo!"

"Mo-jo! Mo-jo! Mo-jo!" the crowd chanted.

"Without further ado, the legendary Legs Flanders and Wheezy

Beevers! Get your mojo workin'!"

With his fingers teasing out an introduction, Wheezy leaned into his microphone. "My bandmate through the decades...my best friend...Legs Flanders and his magic harmonica!"

The crowd whooped and whistled as Legs lumbered to the stage, lazy loops of fog churning in his wake. He moved toward the tall stool and microphone in front of the piano. Wheezy reached out to him. They banged knuckles.

Legs nodded to the drummer to start the beat. He sat and rested one of his Hush Puppies on the lowest rung. Resembling a praying mantis, Legs hunched over the microphone with the harmonica tucked in his hands. A combination of grace and instinct took over. The world disappeared as he closed his eyes.

A slow riff oozed from the instrument, a tease of the genius to come. Legs held one long, fluttering note. He brought down his hand. Wheezy and the band erupted into "Got Your Mojo Workin'."

Spence and Bill beamed with pride as the crowd bounced on the parking lot asphalt. Rick Rakin rocked to the primal beat, his aviator sunglasses flashing a reflection in time with the rhythm. Jean couldn't help but start to dance in the wings.

As Wheezy's fingers whirled over the keys, he leaned into the microphone and shouted, "Get out here, Jean!"

Abandoning her embarrassment, Jean wiggled her hips, bit her lower lip, and shimmied from the wings toward Wheezy. She turned in a circle, whirling her hands as if gathering string.

"Jean, Jean, the dancin' machine!" Wheezy shouted as his black wingtips, never touching the pedals, swished like two baby ducks giving chase to their momma. "Look at her go!"

Legs's hands blurred as if they were wings on a hummingbird, soaring the melody over the driving beat. Lost in the music, he started the grand finale with his frenzied solo.

Sprays of rainbow colors shot from the harmonica and flashed over the stage. Sparkling gold beams and blue threads of ball lightning crackled and bounced around the band, exploding like fireworks when they hit the fog of dry ice. The crowd *ooh*ed and *ahhh*ed at the effect with hundreds of cell phones held high. Legs didn't open his eyes; Wheezy's widened as his mouth popped in shock.

Jean stopped in mid-twirl. A pulsing blue ball of light buzzed her head and shot out over the crowd. The magnetic hum of its path drew her stunned gaze to Spence. He stood frozen in the wings next to Bill, the beer bottle stuck to his lips. His wide eyes locked on hers.

Bill cupped his hands around his mouth. From the edge of the stage, he shouted, "Jean! You got those gels worked out! That's hot!"

CHAPTER 9

How Low Can You Stoop?

Jon Segert stood with Dillon near the catering truck. Like the Collinses, he couldn't help but feel protective. The combination of Dillon's youth—only twenty—and talent rivaling the Old Masters inspired Jon to push harder to achieve his own aspirations. Pride entered into the equation too. He'd been successful in arranging a job for Dillon at the FBI when he finished art school.

"You ready to go to DC? Only a few months away," Jon said.

"As I'll ever be. I'm kind of nervous, though." Dillon pushed his long brown hair behind an ear and stuck his hands in his pockets of his baggy Levis.

"Don't be. You know more than most of the agents on the Art Crime Team already. They'll teach you the rest. To do the job, you need to crawl around in the heads of criminals who have a different passion for art."

"The ugly side."

"Yes, but no less fascinating. Crimes are solved by getting into the core of motivation. Once you've identified that nugget, then you play with it."

"Sounds sinister."

"Nothing different than what an artist does to capture a soul in paint."

"Good point." Dillon went silent, ruminating over Jon's advice.

Jon took a bite of his taco and scanned the passing faces out of habit. He swallowed hard when he spotted Doc and a companion, also immortal, emerging from the crowd. The watch chain on Doc's vest glinted in the sunlight. The shine of his wild gray hair made Jon smile. The impressive black man next to him was unfamiliar, but he too had a wispy outline.

"Quite a noise, Mr. Segert," Doc said, holding out his hand. Jon gave it a warm shake. Dillon leaned into Doc's embrace. "And this young man here is going to set the art world ablaze quite soon."

"He certainly is," Jon agreed.

"And this is Jess." Doc turned and shaded his eyes.

"How do?" Jess said, dipping his head and extending his large hand. Jon was taken aback at the strength of the man's grip.

"A lot of fuss going on up there. Jess told me all about Legs and Wheezy. And I do like to keep tabs on Jean and Spence…and my dog. An important day." Doc threw Jon a mischievous smile, but the contrast of the transparent outline around Jess's dark skin drew Jon's gaze. Fascinating. He wanted to touch it.

Jon shook himself back in the moment. "Spence tells me you're a music buff."

"Could say, I suppose. I seen many of the greats in my days before and after." Jess nodded to Wheezy on stage. "Been a long time since I heard that. He's good."

Doc leaned in to Jon and pointed. "I believe you're acquainted with the unsavory man over there."

Jon followed the trajectory from the end of Doc's finger. Like a laser, his bright blue eyes locked on Nash Winthrop. No mistaking his gelled, curly hair and designer shirt. He'd even pressed his black jeans. A bit of a joke for a man in his fifties.

Jon tossed his plate in the garbage. "What's he doing here?"

"Up to some foolery, I assure you." Doc peered over his wire-rimmed glasses. "Thought you might want to know."

"Should I get him, Mr. Segert?" Jess chuckled. "I can scare him if I show myself."

"No. Let's see what he does."

"I believe I'll head back to Richmond," Doc announced. "You staying behind, Jess?"

"Little while. Can't miss Legs and Wheezy. Gotta tell Spence he done good."

"Suit yourself." Doc faded and disappeared. Jon swished his hand through the smoky remains for a clearer view of Nash.

"I'll keep an eye out with you, Mr. Segert. Don't want nothin' to happen."

"I appreciate your help, Jess. I need more eyes with this many people. You too, Dillon." Jon figured he could use an immortal bouncer right now.

As Legs took the stage, Jon had to bob and weave around the heads of the audience to keep Nash in view. The shouting and whooping became a distraction as people pushed toward the stage.

Nash blended in with the crowd as he moved forward. He appeared to be on a mission. "Stay here," Jon said to Dillon and patted his shoulder.

"I follow you." Jess's deep voice turned serious.

The flash of colors radiating from Legs's harmonica stopped them short. Jon's mouth gaped at what appeared to be arcing electricity. Something didn't seem right about the effect.

"You do that?" he asked Jess.

"Not of my doing. And surely not of this world."

"Ever seen such a thing?"

"The music is a talkin', yes, it is."

Silence hung over the audience after the song ended. Nobody moved a muscle. The light show ceased the moment Legs pulled the harmonica away from his mouth. Then the crowd erupted with applause and whistles. In an instant, dozens of fans had jumped on the stage to line up for autographs. Wheezy hopped off the stool and took a bow. The group surrounded them both, blocking Jon's view. Nash had disappeared.

"Clear this area! Get back!" Jon hoisted himself up on the

platform and signaled for two Milwaukie police officers to help him. "Off the stage!"

"I don't mind," Legs said, signing his name to a festival flyer.

"It's not you I'm worried about!"

"Are you concerned for me?" Wheezy asked, tugging on Jon's shirtsleeve. "Who are you?"

Jean bolted toward the group, her confused expression melted to deep concern. "He's a friend of ours. He's with the FBI." She turned. "What's the matter, Jon?"

"They can sign autographs. I have no issue with that," Spence said.

"Whoa! FBI? I didn't do it, whatever it was!" Wheezy held up his hands.

"You don't look like a Fed-man," Legs said and chuckled.

"Not you! I'm looking for that guy in the white shirt and black jeans...fifties, skinny, dark eyes, wet-looking hair."

"I don't know." Jean gaze scanned the stage. "But where's the harmonica, Legs?"

Nash Winthrop pushed his way through the crowd with a lasered gaze on the stage. He needed to get up to it before Legs came out. This was almost as good as getting his hands on Lucille, B. B. King's famous guitar. He took a long pull from his beer and shoved closer, bumping the walker of an elderly woman.

"Get out of the way! Legs is coming on, and I can't see." She grimaced and stuck out her chin like a constipated bulldog.

"Give me a break, lady," he chided, pushing forward past the bodies and unknown faces.

The stage was low enough for Nash to peer over the edge. In the wings, Legs stood by the partition with the harmonica in his hand.

Nash had successfully slipped through Jon Segert's net once before. If his luck held, slipping out of this festival with that instrument would put him on a new course, an upwardly mobile course.

Legs loped to the stage with a smile and a wave of the harmonica over his head. Nash's gaze followed it like an eagle soaring over the Columbia River. When Legs put the instrument to his lips and started to play, a place in the Hall of Fame became assured. The man's skill couldn't be denied.

Warm air began to swirl as the frenzied solo erupted. An odd hum, beyond the music itself, filled his chest. Coming from the speakers? Feedback?

"What the hell?" Nash froze as flashes of colored beams shot around Legs as he played. From the crowd's reaction, this was just part of the show. They took pictures on their cell phones. Too stunned to follow suit, he stared with his mouth open.

The hair on his arms stood on end. The air magnetized as orbs of bright blue shot out over his head. He tried to identify their source, but the flashes blinded him as they exploded in the billows of dry ice.

The song ended to thunderous applause. Nash heaved himself up, along with a dozen others who jumped on the platform. Legs stood and shook hands with them in sequence. He set the harmonica on the stool when someone shoved a flyer and a pen at him for his autograph.

Nash couldn't believe his luck. With everyone focused on Legs, the instrument sat unnoticed. He swooped in and snatched it with speed and precision. He slipped it in the pocket of his black jeans. As he moved within the stream of roadies to the backstage, he broke off and bolted down the back stairs.

The fast two-block walk to where he'd parked his Beamer in the residential neighborhood seemed to stretch on for a mile. Every ounce of discipline he could muster slowed his stiff steps.

Act normal. Don't rush. No one knew him. No one had seen him. Any minute the area would be crawling with people leaving the festival. Every step slammed a door. No return. Each block spilled a new emotion. Humiliation. Justification. Resolve. When the car was in sight, he practiced his pitch to Kip.

The stifling heat of the black interior stilled his breath but not the pounding in his chest. Suffocating. The harmonica jammed against his thigh, a cruel reminder of how low he had to stoop to make a buck. He eased it out of his pocket; the metal was warm, as if Legs's breath were still circulating inside the chambers. The engine purred as he pulled from the curb.

CHAPTER 10

Slippin' in the Sheets

"Kip?" the dark-haired party girl cooed as she rolled over in the satin sheets. She wrapped herself in them and slipped on her belly to place her feet on the floor, her arms remaining stretched over the mattress. "I don't wanna go to Club Nino tonight. I wanna go to the Boom Boom Room instead. Saturday night is too crowded at Nino." The slight whine in her voice made her sound like a teenager forced to take a family road trip. Claire was thirty-two—at least that's what she'd said when they'd met two months ago.

Claire's reflection caught Kip's eye in the bathroom mirror. Not the one to meet his elderly mother. Too many curves. Mom wanted to see him with a wholesome, successful wife and a carload of kids. Those girls were plentiful in Seattle, but they didn't fill a dress like Claire.

He'd come a long way since managing drugged-out grunge bands in the eighties. His old clients now wandered the streets of Seattle in a burned-out haze. One insider stock tip from a drunken software engineer with a big mouth had catapulted him into the world of wealth.

Taking a risk to borrow fifty grand, Kip bought stock in the company before the announcement broke about their new graphic design software application. The news churned the tip into two hundred when he dumped the shares after the press conference a week later. That secd money created his hedge fund, Forest Investments. Kip's carefully assembled network of corporate secret spillers attracted investors. In only five years, he'd grown the investment balance to over one hundred million. The windfall of fees, plus his own funds, was used to feed his passion for collecting music memorabilia. Now he counted music idols and celebrities among his clients—and they generated more insider tips. Insiders came to him because Kip shared the wealth with those who gave him information. Fees were paid for each tip that produced profits. With the biggest deal yet in the pipeline, he needed help to get more cash in the door.

"Not a chance, Claire." Kip flexed his arms in the bathroom mirror and rolled a sport stick in his pit. He ran a hand through his shoulder-length highlighted hair. After getting the body wave, he resembled Peter Frampton, circa 1977. "Two prospective investors are meeting us at Nino in about forty-five minutes. Plus, one of them has some rare Hendrix stuff. Doll yourself up."

"I need more time…at least an hour to get dressed and do my makeup."

"It'll take two seconds to pour your boobs into the outfit I bought you today. The Jag is leaving in thirty-five minutes." Of course he'd wait for her, if she pushed back—arm candy always sweetened the deal—but she never pushed back. "I'll be downstairs."

The long, curved staircase of steel rail and wire led to the entryway set with naturally shaped river rock. He ran his hand along the polished wood wall of maple inlaid with ebony. The Warhol silkscreen of Mick Jagger greeted him from inside its shadow-box frame at the base of the steps. His latest prize. The open dining room led to a pristine kitchen of maple cabinetry and steel appliances, appreciated only by caterers. Kip didn't cook. This modern home, set among the trees, had been built for entertaining.

His cell phone buzzed in a frenzied circle on the polished concrete countertop. He checked the number and rolled his eyes: Nash Winthrop.

"Forrester."

"Hey, buddy, it's Nash."

"I'm not your buddy—not your anything. Our sweet little deal is over."

"Not quite. I have something you might find interesting. What about vintage blues?"

"I won't guarantee I'm listening."

"Are you interested in Muddy Waters and Legs Flanders?"

Kip paused and licked his lips. "Maybe."

"A harmonica. Played by both of them. Got it this afternoon. Muddy's initials are carved on the mouthpiece. For sale as of today."

"How much?"

"Seventy-five grand."

Mulling over through the possible auction valuations for such a prized artifact, Kip actually thought the price was fair. Two blues legends for the cost of one. A debut of the instrument at his party next week would liven up the atmosphere. The band he'd scheduled played jazz. But he'd trusted Nash before, and that bet had been a losing one.

"I want to see it first," he stalled. "E-mail me a picture right now. Hang up, send it to me, and I'll call you back."

Kip set his phone on the counter and waited. He wanted verification that Nash had the instrument in his possession. Nash might actually be useful; out of a job with an itch in his belly to prove himself as a player. The harmonica would never hit the market. The phone buzzed the arrival of an e-mail. He snatched up the phone and opened the attachment. Outstanding. Dents, dings, and the initials were clearly visible. He called Nash.

"Pretty nice, huh?"

"Fifty thousand," Kip offered. "Not a penny more."

"Sixty thousand and hire me to work with your investment fund," Nash countered. "I'll find you new clients."

Kip needed more investors for this upcoming deal. Nash was just hungry enough to deliver. He let an extra moment of silence hang between them.

"I'll start right away," Nash added.

"Come to Seattle. Bring the harmonica. We'll talk. There's a deal brewing that could be huge. You can show me your prospect list."

"When?"

"Wednesday. We'll meet with the guy who's running a trial on a new drug. I'll e-mail you directions to the restaurant. I need to move fast before the public announcement. And Saturday there's a party at my place—I need the harmonica for that. You deliver, you have a job."

"And you have a harmonica."

Nash hit the end button and swallowed hard. He turned and stared at the harmonica sitting on the maple coffee table. This morning the instrument was a fantasy, and now it was here. The whole afternoon was a blur.

The lazy current of the Willamette River had a hypnotizing effect as he stood at the floor-to-ceiling window in his loft. He followed a sailboat's course toward the Fremont Bridge. The bright sun skipped along the ripples of its wake. He'd moved into this expensive twentieth-floor one-bedroom loft in downtown Portland for the panoramic view. After Wednesday he might be able to make the rent. At least he was better off than his college buddy, Raleigh Coulter. Something never did add up with his death. And his discussion with the FBI afterward didn't add up, either. Screw Jon Segert and his witch hunt.

A wicked prickle raced across the nape of his neck. Nash turned and scratched the skin at the base of his wavy hair. He blinked several times to regain focus. The couch seemed to blur and move. A breeze of heat flushed his face. He rubbed his eyes. When he opened them, a large black man stood in his living room. His overalls and T-shirt had a slight blue cast around them, which intensified against his dark skin. Flecks of gray were dispersed through his thinning hair, but it was hard to tell with the slight illumination around his face. Even though older, maybe seventy, the man looked like he could kick Nash's ass.

"What you gonna do with the harmonica?" the deep voice said. A hint of sarcasm finished the question.

"I...uh...who are you? How did you get in here?"

"Name's Jess. I can go just about anywhere I want. Now, I wanna stick right with you."

"Leave! Out!"

Nash convinced himself the man had been hiding in his apartment when he got home. He'd probably overheard his phone conversation and was trying to extort money. An exercise in futility.

"Doin' nothin' of the sort. You and me, we're gonna get to know one another after you make a call." The man's voice seemed to be coming from every corner of the room, like the sound in a 3D movie theater.

"Call who?" Nash asked, more curious than frightened.

"Jon Segert. Tell him you got Legs's harmonica."

The mention of Sergert's name filled him with panic. He'd not mentioned anything about the agent in his conversation with Kip.

"Well, that's not in the cards!" Nash's eyes went wide. The man disappeared. "What the—" Nash whipped his gaze around the loft. Jess reappeared five seconds later, only three feet away from Nash.

"Told you I can go anywhere. Now take that little telephone in your hand and make it right. Ask him to come here 'cause you want to talk about a harmonica. You don't, then I will."

Nash shifted his wild eyes between Jess and the door. Instinct told him to flee. He lunged, but stopped short as Jess appeared in front of him and grabbed his arm. Nash stared into his endless face in horror.

"Who...what are you?"

"You ready to call? Mr. Segert saw you at the concert. He knows you got it. I'll bet he be comin' here anyhow." The grip of the man's enormous hand tightened and pulled Nash into a head lock.

"Are you FBI?" he choked.

"Let's just say I'm on loan for the afternoon. Your lucky day."

"Does...this have anything...to do with...that talon?" Nash stammered, the blood draining from face.

"I'm no hawk. I'm a man—not your kind. My kind."

Jess seemed to hold him without effort. His arms were vice grips. The man ripped the cell phone from Nash's fist and pushed him away. Nash stumbled into the living room chair as he fell backward. Jess moved to stand in front of the door and stared at Nash's mobile, almost as though he didn't know what to do.

The phone buzzed. Jess studied the screen.

"Why, looka here. Seems Jon Segert is tryin' to talk to *you*." Jess struggled with the device and hit several buttons before answering. A slight halo reflected off his bright white teeth as he smiled. "Jess here, Mr. Segert. I got him. You better get to his place fast as you can."

Jon completed his cruise around the neighborhood surrounding the concert, trying to spot Nash. The streaming crowds leaving the festival should have slowed Nash's ability to make a hasty exit. He pulled the Crown Victoria into the emptying parking lot. Nash. The weasel had worn out his last nerve.

The air conditioner whirred in the idling car. Where would Nash go? He wouldn't drive back to his apartment. Too obvious. Too stupid.

The chief needed an update. He'd be mighty interested in Nash Winthrop being back in the picture. He picked up his cell phone.

"Nash is at it again, Chief. I'm at the Collinses' jazz concert. I can't believe he had the gall to show up here. And even worse, he stole Legs Flanders's harmonica from the stage."

"I'm basting my ribs, Segert, and you want to talk about a damned harmonica? Next you're going to call me that your bike was stolen. It's Saturday, for God's sake!"

"He's up to something. And I'm sure this has to do with Kip

Forrester."

"Forrester's the one you're after, anyway. Forget Nash." The sizzle on the grill punctuated the silence. "Why don't you call him?" The chief laughed like he'd told a brilliant joke. "He might just answer."

Jon rolled his eyes. "Not funny."

As he hung up, his gaze followed a large woman marching down the sidewalk in a bad choice of shorts. Maybe they used to fit. She carried a folding lawn chair with a cell phone planted against her ear. Before he went to the trouble of tracking Nash's mobile on GPS, he decided to give the simple route a try.

"Oh, what the hell."

Jon scrolled through his saved contacts and pressed the number. He didn't expect an answer. On the third ring, his jaw had dropped when he Jess's voice came on the line.

"Stay there! I'm on my way!"

Jon squealed the tires as he tore out of the parking lot, honking to get people out of the street. He turned north on McLoughlin Avenue. He was starting to believe he couldn't do his job without immortal help.

CHAPTER 11

He's Really in There?

The truck carrying the Steinway rounded the corner and disappeared. Senior community buses had raised their ramps and eased down the street in a caravan, their occupants, no doubt, still chattering about the show. The stage had been torn down with lightning speed, the pieces of which were being loaded in the truck. Bill and Linda remained behind to supervise the dismantling of the festival space. Spence waved to them as he started the engine on the RV with Jean, Legs, and Wheezy in the back. Jean started to cry as he pulled out for the five-minute drive down River Road to the house.

"Just a harmonica. Won't make no difference," Legs said, trying to comfort her.

"G-man's on a mission, Jean. He was pissed," Wheezy added. "He'll find it. No blubbering. You look like a raccoon."

Jean sniffed and wiped the smudged mascara from under her eyes as Spence turned into the driveway.

"C'mon, kiddos," Spence urged. "Let's go inside and take a breather."

At home they found cool and quiet, a relief from the heat, the crowds, and the devastating loss of Legs's harmonica. In retrospect, Jean had to admit staging a concert was more work than both she and Spence had bargained for, but the event had been a triumph for the store, and the finale had blown everyone away...literally. The theft, however, blighted their joy.

"Some bad people out there, Music Man," Legs said to Spence. He lowered himself on the couch next to Wheezy.

"I'm so sorry, guys." Spence sat on the opposite love seat. "I had no idea something like this would happen."

"I'll kill the twerp. Let me at him." Wheezy slipped off his wingtips and motioned for Spence to push the hassock closer. He put his feet up and flexed his toes in his black socks. "My dogs are barrrrrr-*king*."

"You're right, Wheezy. I have no doubt Jon will find the harmonica." Jean plunked down in one of the leather club chairs. She set her head back. "I'm beat. My hips hurt."

Wheezy covered his ears. "Don't tell me what you and Spence were doing in our camper, Jean."

"No...from *dancing*."

"You guys were smoking up the stage today," Spence said, his mood brightening. "Ready for some signing sessions when the store opens tomorrow? The whole week will be dedicated to the two of you."

Legs's eyelids grew heavy. "I'll be ready after some shut-eye. Quite a gig."

"Let's not push them, Spence."

"I'm still seeing stars with those light effects you did, Jean. How'd you do that?" Wheezy said, leaning back in the cushions.

Jean glanced at Spence. Their eyes locked. He shrugged.

"You want to tell them?" Spence tapped his front tooth with his fingernail. "Wiley's already been in their bedroom. Only a matter of time."

Legs and Wheezy lifted their heads from the cushions, curious as to her explanation. Jean hesitated and pushed her blond hair behind her ears. She leaned forward.

"Legs? Remember when I took your hands before you went onstage?" She laced her fingers together.

"I do. Some stuff goin' on there like I never seen."

"Me neither. I didn't mean to do it, but something happened when I touched your hand as you held the harmonica. Up until now, only Mary Coulter's possessions have yielded strange effects."

"Who's Mary Coulter?" Wheezy asked.

"Another story for another time," Spence interjected.

"Legs, I transferred magic into you…through the harmonica," Jean continued. "Or maybe…you and the harmonica…to me."

Silence settled over the living room. Wheezy broke the quiet with a laugh.

"Set your hands on my feet, woman. They could use some magic right now."

"No, I'm serious, Wheezy." Jean blew out a breath. "Last year we found an Egyptian piece of cloth in an old trunk I bought from an estate sale. Mary Coulter's estate sale. That's who Mary is—was—*is*, I mean." Jean scrunched her eyes to slow down. "Turns out, the cloth was from Nefertari's tomb and possesses powers…to make people immortal."

Two pairs of eyes bulged with inquisition.

"You full-a nighttime stories, Miss Crazy Eyes." Legs waved his hand and shook his head. "Kids be wettin' their drawers with that one."

"The man in the portrait on the wall is immortal." Jean pointed to Doc's painting. "Born in the mid-1800s. He was at the concert today, talking to the FBI agent we introduced you to, Jon Segert."

"You need therapy," Wheezy scoffed. "Where's that giant cat? I want to put him under my feet."

"I'll prove it." Jean raised her eyes to the ceiling and called out, "Mycroft? Wiley?"

Mycroft lumbered down the stairs and sat, blinking as he studied the group in the living room. The air rippled next to him as Wiley's image materialized. The dog wagged his tail, throwing off sparks in its wake.

"You seein' what I'm seein', Wheez?" Legs elbowed Wheezy.

"Yeah. Crazy times…that's what I'm seeing." Wheezy took off

his thick-framed glasses and rubbed his eyes.

"Watch what they do." Jean stood and stepped to the painting and addressed the animals. "You two want to visit Doc?"

Wiley bounded down the steps into the living room and sat in front of the painting. He waited for Mycroft to follow before he leaped into the canvas and licked Doc's hand.

"Go on, Mycroft. You can get in too."

The cat moved to jump but didn't. He gazed at Jean with an expectant expression, as if he wanted her to help him. Jean tried to hide her concern.

"Want an easy lift?" She picked up the cat and held him in front of Doc's lap. Mycroft extended his paw, crawled inside the painting, and stretched out over Doc's knees. "He's never needed help before." She glanced at Spence.

"Wiley is Doc's dog," Spence said, skipping over Jean's comment. "Mycroft isn't immortal but he has the magic inside him from lying on the fabric. We transformed Doc's adopted daughter last year when we set our hands on it. That was Mary Coulter. We don't fully understand the scope of the power, but we hold its enchantment inside us."

"You ain't kiddin' around?" Legs stood to his full height and took tentative steps to the portrait. He poked his long finger at Mycroft's image like he was a hot coal. Mycroft's paw came out of the painting and batted it. "He inside!"

"Yes, he is," Spence continued. "We think the magic makes choices once the fabric is used to make a worthy person immortal. Now we have a relationship with Mary Coulter's whole ghostly family. They're quite nice. I'm sure you'll meet them at some point."

"And we share Wiley, Doc's retriever. Born in 1913…almost a hundred now. He loves Mycroft." Jean raised her eyes to Legs. "I didn't do the light show—your music did. Your talent—maybe from both of you—ignited the electricity from inside me."

"Never seen nothin' like it in my life," Legs whispered. "For real, I haven't, no I haven't."

"Touch mine, Jean!" Wheezy reached out and wiggled his fingers. "I want to see what you did with Legs."

Jean stepped to Wheezy and held out her hands. He grasped them and squeezed. Within a few seconds, he turned to Legs and opened his mouth but nothing came out. Jean closed her eyes and did the same.

"Ella…" she whispered. "You're playing the piano for Ella Fitzgerald. Smoky light. She's singing 'Bewitched, Bothered, and Bewildered.' Voice of an angel. Lovely fingerwork, Wheezy." Jean released from him and touched the pearls in her earlobes. "These were hers."

"That's right," Legs said, nodding. "Gave 'em to you."

"A gig for the books," Wheezy said. His eyes watered as his thoughts floated away. "I think about that one every day. Damn, I miss her like hell."

"Right with ya, Wheez. Magic too."

"I just know we'll get the harmonica back. We have a secret weapon."

At six o'clock on Saturday evening, Jon whirled through the revolving door of the high-rise apartment building in the Pearl District. He had his credentials out, expecting to run into a security guard in the sleek, modern lobby. When he found no one stationed at the concierge desk, he tucked his billfold back in his pants pocket. The real estate slump had consequences, and one of them was the slashing of budgets for security. He stepped to the shiny steel doors of the elevator. Fingerprints smudged the edges. The cleaning staff had been cut back too.

The button for the twentieth floor glowed yellow. His ears popped just before the doors parted. The hall was empty and quiet. Nobody wanted to be inside on a warm, sunny day in Portland. The tenants must be down at the waterfront park, listening to music at the Saturday Market.

Jon knocked on apartment number 20D, a bit harder than he had intended. He checked both sides of the hallway. All quiet. When the door opened, he stared into the milky outline of Jess, backlit in an orange glow from the setting sun through a large expanse of glass.

"C'mon in, Mr. Segert. A thief in here for ya." Jess smiled and waved him inside.

Nash sat on the couch with the expression of a cornered animal plotting his escape.

"Thanks for holding him." Jon patted Jess on the shoulder. He stopped and stared at Nash. "You ruined a perfectly good day. Now that pisses me off."

Silence. Nash locked his lower jaw in the stubborn position.

"He ain't said much, but then he ain't moved much either." Jess shut the door and crossed his arms.

Jon gazed around the apartment. Expensive. The low-slung modern couch, upholstered in bright orange wool, sat on short steel legs. A vase of deep cobalt-blue glass stood in the center of a bird's-eye maple coffee table. The floor lamps were made of crinkly white paper, like a Japanese lantern. Beyond Nash's head was an expansive view of the Willamette River. Nash didn't deserve this vista in any kind of weather.

"How you paying for all this, Nash? Behind on the exorbitant rent?"

"He not talkin'." Jess stood like a bouncer, the harmonica gripped in his hazy hand. Nash wasn't going anywhere.

"Okay, Chatty Cathy, let's pull your string." Jon sat on the bright orange bucket chair shaped like a concave cough drop. The buttons on the seat poked the back of his thigh. "Why'd you steal the harmonica?"

Nash shook his finger to Jess. "What the hell is that guy? He gives me the heebies. I want a lawyer. I'm pressing charges for assault."

"Ah...he speaks! Remember when I appointed one for you in our interview last year? Goes by Horus?" Jon took out the talon and set it on the coffee table. "Jess is kind of like the hawk, only meaner." Inside, he chuckled. Jess wouldn't hurt a flea.

Nash's eyes went wide as he stared at the talon, clearly reliving the events of the claw's transformation during their discussion about Raleigh Coulter.

"Do *not* lay your crazy sci-fi crap on me, Agent Segert." Nash leaned away from the table.

"I won't if you tell me what you're planning to do with the harmonica." Jon turned to Jess, who stood by the front door.

Jess smiled and held up the instrument. Daylight from the picture window glinted off the metal. "Got it right here." He stepped to the chair and handed it to Jon.

"Okay, Nash, we're off to a good start." Jon smoothed his hand over the carved letters. "But what's the bigger plan at work in that mighty, pea-size brain of yours? The neighbors wouldn't appreciate you playing 'Yankee Doodle Dandy' on this all night."

"I was going to sell it." Nash grimaced. A hint of embarrassment had crept into his voice.

"To whom? Surely not on eBay or Craigslist."

Silence.

"Hmmm…let's say"—Jon opened his hands in an exaggerated gesture—"Kip Forrester?"

Nash blew out a breath, all of his conceived plans streaming out with it. "Look. This isn't about the harmonica." Nash put his elbows on his knees and rubbed his face. "I need money and a job."

"Don't we all." Jon studied Nash's expression. The lines of a fifty-something-year-old around his eyes had seemingly deepened and catapulted him to sixty-something since Jon had last seen him. "Tell me why."

"Kip collects famous instruments."

"And this will get you in good with him?" Jon inspected the mouth holes on the harp. A sacrilege for it to be used as a greedy bargaining chip.

"Something like that."

"What's he doing for you that you'd take such a risk? Stealing this harmonica was a bonehead move—pretty lowlife, Nash." A plan gathered steam in Jon's mind.

"Big deal brewing. He's going to hire me to help him find investors."

"What kind of *deal?*"

"Nooo way! Uh-uh. Telling you would violate the confidentiality of Kip's business." Nash held up his hands in defense.

"Isn't that a bit hypocritical, Winthrop? Seems to me you had no trouble violating those ethics at VEY Steel." Jon stared down Nash in the silence. "What? Did you drink from the chalice of honor in the last two hours?"

"Work with me here, Segert." Nash rubbed his forehead.

"How about you work with me instead?" Jon let his words float between them. Nash raised his eyes. Jon gave his words a nudge over the coffee table. "I think Forrester is going to jail as soon as I have proof of his insider game. And if you get on the wrong side of this investigation, you'll be eating beans right beside him."

"What do you mean? Kip's legitimate." Nash shifted to avoid eye contact and studied the crease in his jeans.

"C'mon, Nash. What's he said to you about this potential deal?"

"I don't know anything yet. I won't find out until Wednesday. He wants me to meet with him and a pharmaceutical guy at a restaurant in Seattle. Then he's got some big party at his house on Saturday. I promised him the harmonica. Without that, I'm hosed out of a job."

"Next week?" Jon studied the crudely scratched letters, *M* and *W*, on each end of the metal plate, authenticating the historic piece. Jon made a silent apology to it for what he was about to do.

"Yeah. I'm driving up on Tuesday night."

"Good. Keep the appointment." Jon glanced back at Jess.

"Hope you know what you doin', Mr. Segert." He faded to nothing. Jon waited until the residual haze dissipated.

Shock washed across Nash's face. In a shaky voice, he said,

"That's the third time he's disappeared. Is that some virtual technology you FBI types developed?"

"Yeah, a hologram. Pretty nifty, huh? You won't have to worry about him if you cooperate. But if you don't..."

Nash eyed him, skeptical. He rubbed his arm from the virtual grip. "I'm worried about a lot of things, Agent Segert. And right now I'm questioning my sanity."

Jon turned the harmonica over in his hand, deliberating as to whether his idea would work. He handed the harmonica to Nash. "Here. Take this and sell it to Kip as you originally planned." Jon picked up the talon from the coffee table and flicked the needled point.

Nash's gaze shifted to the curved claw as his fingers tightened around the instrument.

"Is this another one of your tricks?"

"No. Not a trick, but I need your help."

"What do I have to do?"

"Wear a wire."

CHAPTER 12

The Trees are so Green

On the following Wednesday morning, Anhur glanced out the window of the private jet and marveled at the orange glow. The rising sun hit the frozen cap on Mount Hood like a fireball. Lose a day; gain a new world. Crossing time zones took a toll on his mental clarity. Generous board members fully supported his taking the fabric out of harm's way in Cairo, but he wasn't so sure about this Agent Dan Brick. It had taken much effort to convince the FBI agent that an escort was unnecessary. Distrust, when combined with ignorance of the fabric's power, was a dangerous proposition. In misplaced hands, the artifact might become quite deadly, much more deadly than the protesters in Tahrir Square.

The jet started a steep descent. He patted the metal-sided briefcase in the leather seat next to him and checked to make sure the flash drive was safe in the breast pocket of his suit jacket. Out of necessity, he may need to expose its secrets.

The flight attendant stepped to his seat, one of only six.

"We will be on the ground in ten minutes, Mr. Kumar. Would you care for one last refreshment?" Her broad white smile lit the jet's interior.

"No, thank you, Nailah."

"Very well. You will need to fasten your seat belt for landing. Shall I store the case?"

"Quite all right. I'll keep it here. I cannot let this out of my sight."

The course of the Columbia River ushered their position to the runway of Portland International Airport. The immediate reverse of the engines jerked the six-seat jet to a stop in seconds. Anhur scanned the scene as they rolled to the gate. So green. The hills, lush with vegetation and extravagant homes, enjoyed a view of Mount St. Helens limited only by weather.

Anhur stood with a tight grasp on the briefcase as the door unsealed. Nailah handed him his leather duffel bag.

"We will be on standby, Mr. Kumar. When you are ready to return, we will be at the hotel."

He bowed his head and exited through the doorway.

A tall, square-jawed man waited for him at the bottom of the stairs. His expression betrayed no emotion, unlike most Americans'. In fact, the man's eyes were all but invisible. They were two thin slits, as were his lips. His chestnut hair seemed to be carved from wood.

"Special Agent Dan Brick." The man shouted over the whine of the engines and extended his hand. No smile. No warm welcome. Anhur didn't believe the man had laughed in quite a while.

"Anhur Kumar." He thought it best to match the agent's stiff tone. An image of two circling male dogs in defense of a purebred beauty filled his mind. This could be a greater challenge than he anticipated. "May I drop my belongings at the hotel? I'm staying nearby."

"Good idea. The hotel is a better place for us to meet, anyway. You have the artifact, right?"

"Yes, Agent Brick. I would not have flown thirteen hours with empty hands."

Anhur ushered the agent into his spacious suite at the Hyatt Place. His assistant had chosen this hotel because of its proximity to the airport and the FBI offices. It's modern, comfortable style offered all the conveniences of home, including a sitting area with a sleek L-shaped couch, the color of dried wheat, and a chocolate-brown leather hassock. The sleeping area was behind a half wall, paned with opaque glass framed in dark-stained wood. A fully appointed desk area and built-in bar were located across from the sitting area. Anhur set the case on the leather hassock, but this would not be a relaxed conversation. Anhur sensed Brick's gaze following him as he switched on every lamp in the room.

The emotion he had felt talking with Mary Coulter in Cairo eclipsed his trepidation of this meeting. Actually conversing with an immortal reduced a conversation with a mortal to mere pedestrian annoyance. And being on the cusp of revealing the fabric's secrets had an energizing effect, pushing aside his jet lag. Anhur stepped to the bar counter and reached for a large bottle of Pellegrino water, making the trapped bubbles fizz when he twisted the cap. Without raising his eyes, Anhur filled two glasses and handed one to the FBI agent.

"Agent Brick, I do not believe you have any idea what you are delving into in your investigation."

"I know I'm dealing with something that defies explanation. I'm counting on you to enlighten me." Dan took a sip of the water and swished it in his mouth to release the bubbles.

"I would like to call Jean and Spencer Collins. They should be made aware I am here."

"They'll be told soon enough. I want to get filled in on this thing first."

"How much time is at your disposal?"

Anhur set his phone on the desk and slipped his jacket over the chair. He gave the breast pocket a squeeze. He unbuttoned the cuffs of his crisp white shirt and turned up the sleeves.

"As much as I need." Brick sat on the couch and rested his elbows on his knees. "I appreciate the long way you traveled to show me this artifact." Brick stared at the case.

"Your subpoena ensured this was not a favor." Anhur took a

seat on the extended section of the couch and set one hand on the aluminum briefcase. "I'm afraid even I do not fully comprehend the fabric's secrets."

A slight smile crossed Brick's face and disappeared. "Try me."

"I assume you want to inspect the piece?"

Brick grimaced, his response to the question.

"Yes, of course you do. My one condition is that you must guarantee you will help me to keep this protected, not only for the monetary value—which cannot begin to be calculated—but for its power. I agreed to your request because of the urgency to remove the fabric from possible harm, or worse yet, theft. Cairo is not safe." *And for Mary Coulter,* he added in his mind.

"You don't set conditions, Mr. Kumar—I do." The agent set his glass on the side table. He moved to release the buckles.

"No! Please!" Anhur paused to compose himself. "It is specially wrapped inside. Let me relay a bit of history before I remove it."

Brick narrowed his beady eyes and set his hands in his lap.

"I'm listening."

"The artifact in this case was found in an urn during the excavation of the tomb of Queen Nefertari in 1904. Unfortunately, it was not documented, but I believed, without a doubt, the piece existed. A worker on his team smuggled it out of the country. The Collinses relayed this information to me. The fabric passed through the hands of the Gaines family in Richmond, Virginia, and finally went into ownership of the final descendant, Mary Coulter."

At the mention of the name, Brick straightened in his seat.

"Raleigh Coulter's mother? Didn't she die last year?" Brick shook his finger at Anhur. "Yeah. Right after Raleigh was killed."

"Yes…and no." Anhur stood, drained his glass, and moved to the bar. He refilled and took a large swallow. Now that he'd gone this far, he had to reveal the truth—but not yet. Anhur returned to his seat on the couch.

Brick leaned back on the cushion, crossed his arms, and stared at him. "Where do Jean and Spencer Collins enter into the picture? Did they steal this from Mary Coulter?" He jutted his prominent chin toward the case.

"No, Agent Brick." Anhur scoffed at the thought. "Not thieves. The Collinses found the heirloom in a trunk from her estate sale."

Brick sighed, somewhat disappointed. "You're being cryptic."

"I assure you, they were quite honorable in their motivations."

"How?"

"Knowing it had to be something special, they met with a friend and colleague of mine in London to obtain more information about its origins. Mary's son stole the artifact from Mrs. Collins outside of the Victoria and Albert Museum. His goal was to sell the piece to an antiques dealer. Jean and Spencer attempted to take it back in order to meet with me in Cairo the next morning. Fortune was on their side. Jon Segert was nearby, watching this Raleigh Coulter for a different reason when the event took place."

"Then what? Get to the taxi."

"Raleigh sped away in one with the fabric in his possession. Jean, Spencer, and Agent Segert gave chase in another in order to follow him. The birds—the ones stitched into the fabric—sensed the eminent threat and responded to protect not only the fabric but the Collinses and Mr. Segert."

"What do you mean 'responded'?" Brick narrowed his eyes. "Does this have something to do with the reports of a hawk killing Raleigh Coulter?"

Anhur paused, organizing his thoughts. Brick gave him a quizzical look, waiting for more information. "Jean and Spencer did an important service to my country when they brought the artifact to the Cairo Museum, but most of all to Mary Coulter."

"How? What's this got to do with her?"

"The birds transform, Mr. Brick. They take the dying into immortality. They are phoenixes."

"That's a myth. They don't exist." Brick waved his hand to dismiss the possibility. "C'mon, Kumar. This is ridiculous."

Anhur set both hands on the hassock and leaned toward the

agent. Less than a foot of air stood between their faces. Their eyes locked.

"Jean and Spencer made Mary Coulter immortal."

"What?" Brick's lids widened, revealing deep-olive-green irises. He reached for the water glass and took a hard swallow.

"Everlasting life. She lives. I spoke to her in my office in Cairo before I came here."

"Open the case."

Click. Click.

Anhur lifted a leather-covered bundle from the metal briefcase. He removed the case and set it on the floor. As he opened the pouch, he monitored the man's expression.

"Are you prepared, Agent Brick?"

"For a bunch of mumbo jumbo."

The fabric rested on the hassock, folded, and ready to reveal secrets. Tension filled the hotel room as Anhur pulled back each corner.

Brick sucked in a breath. He stared, taking in the brilliant, iridescent colors.

"Your phoenixes." Anhur smiled, triumphant, appreciating the reaction. His goal of breeding respect for the relic had been achieved.

The smooth fabric glittered with the images of three birds. Luminous sprays of red, gold, green, and turquoise radiated from their feathers in the warm glow from the lamp. A trio of small black eyes blinked in a random pattern.

Brick's hand shook as he reached out, as if it drew his touch. "What the—this transforms?"

"Do not give in to the temptation," Anhur whispered.

"But—"

"No, Agent Brick. They are alive. What is your true character?"

"The truth. That's all I want."

"Are you worthy of the truth?"

"Of course!"

"We shall see. The phoenixes are judges in these matters."

Anhur turned the fabric by the corners to face Brick, who stared in silence, drinking in the details of the birds, vines, and small white flowers.

"Quite magnificent, yes?" Anhur said.

"Did these birds kill Raleigh Coulter?"

"Not in their present form. Only the Collinses and your colleague, Jon Segert, understand what happened to the man in the taxi."

The phoenixes blinked again, their eyes shifting from Anhur to the agent. Brick pulled his hand away as if the images would bite.

"This is nuts. You...you put some kind of computer animation chip in this fabric." Brick pointed and shook his finger. "I've seen...stuff like it on the Discovery Channel."

"I assure you this is no television program."

Brick stood and glared, his face a frozen mix of defiance and denial.

"Be at the FBI offices Friday morning at ten o'clock sharp! I want to talk more, but I need a day to think. Everyone involved— you, me, Jon, and the Collinses—need to sit down and discuss this. In the meantime, I'm going to make arrangements for that thing to be tested."

"Tested for what, might I ask?"

Brick hesitated. "The building is only down the street. The hotel shuttle can bring you to this address." He flicked the corner of his business card.

"As you wish. Would you prefer to call the Collinses, or shall I?"

"Don't you dare. I will."

Brick slapped the card on the side table next to his empty glass.

He pointed to Anhur from the doorway. "If...if I find out you're in on this charade, Anhur, you'll be in as much trouble as they're in right now. You'd better not be screwing with me."

The door hissed closed and latched behind the agent.

Anhur took a sip of Pellegrino water. Not quite the response he had anticipated. He eyed his cell phone sitting next to Brick's card.

He called the Collinses' number. His shoulders slumped when the voice mail started an automated greeting.

"Jean and Spencer, this is Anhur Kumar. I have been summoned to Portland by Agent Dan Brick. I am here with the fabric at the Hyatt Place near the airport. I would strongly advise both of you and Jon Segert to make yourselves unavailable for the next few days. The information I must reveal compromises our agreement to maintain confidentiality. Please erase this message. I did not call you."

Dan Brick marched off the elevator at the FBI offices. Faces in the cubicles blurred on his way to his office. He slammed the door. The side window rattled. He threw his keys on the desk so hard they didn't stop moving but slid off the desk to the floor. He blew out a breath and picked them up. He stared at them as Kumar's words flowed through his veins like an injection of adrenalin.

He turned the keys over in his hand. None of this information from Kumar unlocked anything but more questions. Phoenixes? Transformations? Immortality? This was beginning to show shades of a cult or some secret society that used black magic for sacrifices.

Creepy.

All crap. Every bit of Anhur's rehearsed spiel. Crap.

But what if it wasn't?

Dan exited his office and stood in the hallway, forgetting why. Heads poked above the cubicle partitions, curious, watching him.

"Where's Segert?" he called out to no one in particular.

"At his desk, but don't go in. He's on surveillance," Jenny Kowalski's voice said from behind an upholstered partition. Her stay-away tone sounded protective.

"Screw that." Dan proceeded to knock on Jon's closed door, not sure what the hell he would say. Everything seemed like a trap—a setup. And he was the only one not in on the joke.

Dan banged on the window. Jon sat in front of his computer with a pair of headphones on, shooing his hands for Dan to go away.

He stepped inside anyway.

"I need to talk with you. I just met with—"

"Not now, Brick. I'm getting ready to listen to Winthrop. Give me until next week."

"Can't."

"Well, it's going to have to wait, Brick," another voice said.

Dan flinched and turned to the growling voice gripping the back of his neck from the hallway.

"That's an order!" The chief had stepped up behind him in the doorway. "Don't screw with Jon's wire." His eyes seemed to glow hot. "I'm watching you like a hawk."

Dan bristled at the simile. He turned and marched back to his office to review the hospital records of Raleigh's death. The doctor wouldn't talk, and neither would the attending nurses. And now the chief was in on this conspiracy.

CHAPTER 13

The Common Cold

At 4:45 on Wednesday afternoon, Nash pulled into a parking space at the U.S. Bank building on Fifth Avenue in downtown Seattle. He idled the Beamer to keep the blast of cool air going. It wasn't that hot outside, but he raged like an incinerator. The last thing he wanted was to break a sweat. His yellow tie visibly bounced as his heart hammered beneath his white cotton shirt. In fifteen minutes he had to be on the escalator to the Palomino Restaurant above the main lobby. Kip wanted to meet early to do the deal on the harmonica and brief him about their meeting with Dr. Braxton Hughes, head of research for Enzer Pharmaceuticals. He shut off the engine and called Jon.

"How do I know this thing is working?"

"Don't worry—it does. Ignore it. Pretend the microphone doesn't exist. The first step is to make sure the harmonica transaction takes place. Second, just participate in the meeting when Hughes shows up. Don't push or lead the conversation in any one direction. Let them incriminate themselves. If they're legit, knock yourself out in the new job. If not, then you're working for me."

"Nothing else?"

"Offer up investors. I don't care. Just don't tip them off. They'll scream entrapment. I'm only interested in Kip's and the doctor's part of the discussion. You'd better get up to the restaurant."

Nash hung up and flipped over the lapel of his suit jacket. "Testing. I'm going in."

In the lobby of the U.S. Bank building, he studied his image in the window of the Starbucks. At least through today he wasn't working there. Oddly, making the decision to cooperate with the FBI gave him renewed confidence. The scared rabbit routine was getting old. Dodging Jon Segert over the past year had worn him down.

Nash straightened his navy gabardine jacket and smoothed his lapel. The microphone wasn't visible. All good. He stretched his mouth several times to get his face to relax. On the other side of the glass window, a burnout with a blond ponytail and laptop started laughing. The man held up his cappuccino in a mocking toast. Nash's confidence drained out through his toes and pooled inside his tasseled loafers.

As he glided up the escalator from the main lobby, Nash spotted Kip waiting at the reservation podium of the restaurant. The aroma of mesquite and grilled meat hit his nose as he reached the landing. Too nervous to eat. He couldn't miss the psychedelic colors and geometric shapes on Kip's vintage tie. A lapel pin advertised his charter membership in the Rock and Roll Hall of Fame.

"Been a while. Good to see you," he said, extending his hand. "Love the tie." Nash inhaled but couldn't take in a full breath.

Kip turned to the hostess, his countenance all business. "We'll have another gentleman joining us in about twenty minutes. Bald, glasses, tall. A quiet table, please. We're having a meeting."

"Absolutely. Follow me." The woman led Kip and Nash to a high-backed booth upholstered in dark-brown leather. The table was covered with a white linen tablecloth. Images of red horses galloped across paper placemats. Kip slid in on one side, Nash on the other, facing the entrance.

The back of the tight skirt drew Kip's gaze as the hostess did a runway-model sashay back to her station on three-inch heels. He turned back to Nash.

"Mmm-mmm. You got the harmonica with you?"

"Right here." He patted his breast pocket, remembered the microphone, and wondered if the sounds of any shifting he did would prevent Segert being able to hear the conversation. He'd have to be as still as possible, just in case. "Did you bring a check?"

"Let me see it." Kip held out his hands, hungry to hold the vintage steel. A glint filled his eyes. Nash reached in his breast pocket and handed him the instrument.

Kip inspected the carved initials and ran his finger over the mouthpiece. "Damn. A lot of great music came out of these holes, Nash. How'd you get this?"

"I met Legs Flanders when he played in Portland last Saturday. He and Wheezy Beevers were in town for a jazz festival."

"I'm sorry I didn't make it down for that." Kip narrowed his eyes. "I'm going to have this authenticated, but for now I have to trust that you're playing straight with me."

"Oh, it's real all right. I watched Legs play that in person."

"C'mon. Tell me. How much did you pay for it?"

"Rather not say."

Kip pressed his lips together and leaned over the table. "This deal I'm working on is huge. I need to fill you in on what I expect out of you."

"So you want the harmonica? Sixty grand, like we agreed?"

Kip slipped the instrument in his jacket pocket and pulled out a check.

"Here."

Nash put the check in the breast of his suit coat. Fleeting confidence bled through the fibers of pressed paper. "Before we talk about this deal, what's my salary?" Nash started to pick at the cuticle of his thumb. When he pulled a piece of skin that hurt, he stopped. Bleeding in a meeting was a bad idea.

"Commission only. No salary. You get 1 percent of the gain for each investor you deliver." Kip stopped talking when the waitress presented three menus.

"A cocktail until your third guest arrives? Wine?" she offered.

"Gin and tonic, twist of lime," Kip requested.

"Iced tea for me." Nash figured he'd better keep a clear head. *Commission only?* Another month would pass before he'd see another check.

"C'mon! Have a real drink. You're about to become rich."

"No, I have to drive back to Portland tonight. I want to start sending out e-mails and make some phone calls in the morning."

Kip studied him and then said, "Good man. I like that. A worm getting the bird." He laughed at what he thought was a clever retort. "Let's wait to order until Dr. Hughes gets here." Closing the menu, Kip leaned on his elbows. Nash did the same, resisting the temptation to check his lapel.

"I met Braxton at a party a few weeks ago. He's gold. Been working on this whoop-de-doo drug. He wouldn't tell me what. His fee for the information is the equivalent of 10 percent of all my investor's profits one week after the company makes the announcement. Can you believe the gall?"

"When will Enzer make the news public?"

"Next month. You have three weeks to round up as many people as possible to buy shares through the fund. Once the news breaks in the media, the price is going to skyrocket. Then we dump the sucker. Get it?"

"Pricey. Hughes will make a bundle."

"Chump change. We're making some serious coin on this too." Kip winked. "Hughes says this drug might rival penicillin." He raised his eyes to the hand-blown glass light fixture above their table as if the abstract domes could hear their conversation.

They went silent again when the waitress set the drinks in front of them.

Nash picked a sugar packet from the holder and shook it like a lit match. He wanted in on this deal. *Damn Segert.* He froze, realizing the noise might obliterate the conversation. "So, what do you think it is?" Nash asked, emptying the brown grains into his tea.

"That's why we're here. He wouldn't tell me until I agreed to his terms."

"So did you?"

"Damn straight I did."

"Do you have all this in writing?"

Kip scowled as though Nash had just hit the rim of the basket on a layup. "Spit and a handshake. First law of getting rich: Don't leave a trail."

Nash bobbed his head, picturing Jon Segert sticking up his thumb in approval. He spotted a man in his fifties who fit Hughes's description sauntering toward their booth.

"I think he's here," he whispered. "Tall and bald—walking this way."

"Black glasses?"

"Yeah."

Kip appeared nervous as he slid out of the booth and stood. The two men shook hands.

"Brax, this is Nash Winthrop," Kip said. "He's helping me to get investors."

"I like the sound of that." Hughes unbuttoned his jacket and sat next to Nash facing Kip. "I can't stay long." He gazed around the restaurant, probably checking for acquaintances.

"What is this wonder drug, Brax, and why will it be so big?" Kip seemed too anxious. A few niceties would have been more appropriate before the grilling.

Hughes took off his glasses and swung them in a half circle, clearly enjoying the tension secrets deserved.

"What's the one ailment that sickens nearly one billion men, women, and children each year in the United States alone?"

Nash scrolled through the litany of afflictions he'd suffered in the past twelve months: a bee sting, bad Thai chicken, sinus infection, and a sweat rash on his thighs from the gym. He could tell Kip was doing the same thing. They both stared at Hughes, hesitant to be the first to offer an answer.

"Allergies?" Kip blurted out, trying to act smart.

"No." Hughes smirked in the pause. "The common cold."

"Holy crap!" Kip immediately lowered his voice when a woman at a nearby table turned around. "C'mon. Scientists have been trying to come up with a cure for decades. Nobody's been able to find one. How?"

"I developed an immune enzyme that attacks the molecular structure of the cold virus—any strain. It's been in the works for the past five years. The human trials are done. As you know, we went public last year after the successful launch of our antifungal drug. The founders delayed this product coming to market because they wanted their stock options to vest first." Hughes tapped the table. "Everyone on the staff is going to make a bundle when this one hits."

"And the results of the trials?"

"80 percent effective in eliminating the virus if taken within the first twenty-four hours of symptoms."

"What about the other twenty?" Nash interjected, hoping to offer something that would impress Kip. From the look Kip shot him, that wouldn't do it.

"That group consisted of patients with compromised immune systems, such as those with HIV and cancer."

"So tell us what's in this miracle concoction," Kip continued.

"A derivative of the naturally occurring enzyme in colostrum. Mother's milk. That's why newborns don't get sick. Immunities are transferred from the mother to the child. I found a way to synthesize it."

"Isn't colostrum already on the market?" Nash asked. "I think I've seen it at Whole Foods." Kip kicked him under the table.

Hughes gave Nash a dismissive glance. "This formula is better."

"Everybody and his brother will take this stuff," Kip said, glaring at Nash.

"Any side effects?" Nash asked.

"Zero side effects. Even those with dairy allergies can tolerate this. And best of all, it's not a drug—in the legal sense of the word. Tucks right in the supplement category. No waiting game or politics with the FDA. What the company will lose from the formula not being a prescription drug, they'll make up in volume. A bottle of thirty capsules won't be more than twenty-five bucks. That's less than a month's supply of Co-Q 10."

"The stock will go through the roof." Kip nodded his approval.

"Do the math, gentlemen. I'll be buying you lunch in about a month, after the press conference on July twentieth. I trust you won't have any problem rounding up investors by then. Everyone can relate to catching a miserable summer cold."

"I'm buying a block of stock tomorrow morning."

"And the downside of the nondrug route?" Nash squeezed the wedge of lemon in his glass, and a squirt shot across the table. Kip brushed his sleeve.

"We'll be pissing off a lot of doctors. This'll cut into their bread and butter. Complications from the common cold make up a good percentage of doctor visits. I suppose the AMA could try to sue, taking the position the composition of this enzyme should be categorized as a drug. They wouldn't win."

"What's the stock price on Enzer today?" Nash regretted the question. He should have checked the ticker at the market's close.

"Around eight bucks as of this afternoon, but it'll go to eighty when this is announced. According to my calculation, the fee for this information is just over seven a share. Buying now will give investors the best margin." Hughes elbowed Nash. "Don't want you guys cutting into my profits, now."

"You're not under a confidentiality clause?" Nash asked. He shifted when Kip widened his eyes.

"Pffftt. Doesn't mean a thing." Dr. Hughes took off his glasses and wiped them on the corner of the tablecloth.

"Are you ready to order? I'm starved." Kip said, changing the subject.

"Nothing for me." Hughes glanced at his watch. "Got to get back. They want a consult on packaging. All about marketing now." He drummed the table with his forefingers. "You two enjoy yourselves. We won't talk again until after the press conference."

"Wait a minute!" Kip spread his hands. "What's the name of this product?"

"MammaGels." Hughes winked.

He stood and breezed out of the restaurant.

Kip's gaze followed the back of Braxton's tan linen jacket, a waft of thick cologne lingering in his wake. He turned back to Nash and shook his head. "Titty pills?"

"They should put big-breasted women on the label," Nash quipped, sucking at the bottom of his glass. "Huge. I can sell this." He poked at the ice with a straw.

"You *are* coming to my party on Saturday, right? You'll need to help me work the crowd."

"Wouldn't miss it."

The waitress approached the booth with a handheld computer. Nash turned and smiled. "I'll have the Chop-Chop Salad."

"Tuna puttanesca." Kip handed her the menu. As she walked away, Kip lifted his gin and tonic. "Here's to big tits and the god-damned common cold."

Nash lifted his empty glass. "I'll be right back. I have to go to the bathroom."

Jon Segert stayed late into the evening and stared at his computer, digesting the recorded conversation after listening to it for the third time. His gut about the man had been right. Not only was Kip annoy-ing but he proved to be an idiot too. The common cold? Snake oil pills. He replayed the sound file of the whole conversation again because he couldn't believe his ears. Other than the distortion of thirty seconds of loud scratching, paper rustling, and crunching ice, Nash had done a pretty decent job. The recording had everything Jon needed to issue an arrest warrant for Kip Forrester and Braxton Hughes.

The rough numbers he'd written on his notepad estimated

Hughes's take to be upward of four million if Kip and Nash rounded up only thirty big-ticket investors. And, no doubt, each client would buy tens of thousands of shares with the preannouncement stock price so cheap.

Jon tapped his pen on the pad and raised his eyes to the Rolling Stones' *Tumbling Dice* poster, a gift from Spence.

"A gamble with good odds," he muttered. The buzz of his phone interrupted the thought. He checked the number: Nash's mobile.

"Hey. You did well with your first wire."

"My last wire," Nash said. "Nerve-racking stuff. I think I got him to say everything you wanted."

"On the money."

"Now what?"

"Come on back to Portland. Don't get investors, Nash. You'll embroil yourself in complications. Sit tight and tell Kip your prospects will wire funds after the shindig on Saturday. The whole deal will tumble down on Sunday." Jon smirked as he glanced at the poster.

"He paid me, Jon."

"Cash the check as soon as the bank opens. Pay your rent and watch the sailboats."

"What are you going to do?"

"There's a party I haven't been invited to. Off to Seattle on Saturday morning." Jon heard Nash's tense silence. "Don't you, under any circumstances, show up at that party."

"How will I get out of it?"

"Tell Kip you have a cold."

CHAPTER 14

Ain't that just like a G-Man

On the Thursday after the festival, Not Fade Away was packed with collectors and jazz enthusiasts who stood in line to pay for their armfuls of vinyl. Others were in the store to meet Legs and Wheezy for their fourth straight day of signing autographs. Jean kept the line moving; Bill manned the register, while Spence talked up the crowd with tidbits of trivia. Linda alphabetized the stacks on hold from called-in requests.

The opening week had been a raging success. The CD recording from the festival filled the speakers in each corner of the ceiling. A stack of jewel cases with Legs's and Wheezy's pictures on their covers stood in a rack beside the cash register. Wiley stayed behind the counter with Bill.

"You doing okay, Sparkles?" Bill chuckled at his pet name for Wiley. He leaned down and scratched behind the dog's ears.

A young man with sand-colored dreadlocks handed Bill a twenty. "You might have a plug shorting out back there. Something's sparking."

"Selling too many records. Maybe the music's too hot."

The phone rang.

"Jean, can you grab that?" Spence called out over the music. "Bill's got people in line."

"Be right back, Legs." Jean trotted to the counter and picked up the receiver. "Not Fade Away."

"Jon here."

"Hey, Jon! We're tearing up the record world. You should come to the store on Saturday."

"I'm going to Seattle on Saturday."

"What for?"

"To get Legs's harmonica."

"No way!" Jean turned and shouted, "Hey, everybody, Jon found the harmonica!"

"Don't celebrate! We're not done yet. That's not all I'm doing. Let me explain."

"Where is it?"

"When will you guys be home?"

"We close in an hour. Want to come by the house?"

"Sure."

At six thirty, Jon knocked on the pomegranate-colored double doors of Jean and Spence's house. The doorbell was off limits. It scared Mycroft. The wood buzzed with Charlie Parker's sax being played on the stereo inside.

Expecting to be greeted by Jean or Spence, his gaze traveled downward when Wheezy answered the door.

"Howdeeee, G-man! You here to give us good news about the blower?"

"Something like that."

The normally peaceful house was in chaos. Wiley ran down the stairs as Jean whirled around the kitchen making dinner. The volume on the music was turned up too high. Legs stood at Doc's portrait in the living room, trying to tickle Mycroft on Doc's lap. Spence was replacing the liner after taking out the garbage.

"Welcome to Grand Central, Jon," Jean said and added a wine glass to the four already on the counter.

"Let's all sit. I need to fill you in on something. Turn off the stereo." Jon's cell phone rang. He checked the number and silenced the buzz. Brick wasn't going to screw this up.

Wheezy waddled down the steps and settled into his claimed spot on the loveseat. "C'mon Legs! Leave the cat alone."

"He's in there, but I still don't believe what I'm seein'." Legs stepped to the leather chair and shook his head. "You got somethin' for us, Fed-man?"

Jon waited until Spence lifted the stylus from the album. His shoulders lowered two inches in the quiet. Jean gave everyone a glass of wine.

"Jess found Nash with the harmonica," he announced.

"Our immortal Jess? I'll be damned," Spence said, rubbing his chin. "The whole family is getting into the sleuthing act."

Swirling his red wine, Jon hesitated. "But I gave the harmonica back to Nash."

"Are you crazy?" Jean blistered.

"Ain't that like the government," Legs interjected. "Give you somethin' and take it back."

"Yeah! And make you thank them for the honor," Wheezy added, lifting his glass before taking a sip.

"Now wait a minute! This isn't what you think. I'm using it to trap an inside trader who collects famous instruments. Name's Kip Forrester. I let Nash sell it to the guy because Nash agreed to cooperate with me. He wore a wire, so I have the whole transaction recorded. I'm going to Seattle on Saturday to take Forrester and his accomplice into custody. I'll bring the harmonica home with me."

"Just like a G-man," Wheezy said. "Got to make everything complicated."

"How can you do both things by yourself?" Jean leaned forward, interested in the plan.

"Kip Forrester is throwing a big party on Saturday. Jazz musicians will be playing, so I'm sure he'll show off his latest acquisition."

Jon spotted Jean glancing at Spence. He braced himself.

"Why don't Legs and Wheezy make a surprise guest appearance?" she suggested. "They're right here."

"I'll play for 'em and bring the harp on home," Legs said. "Don't want anybody messin' on it, anyhow."

"Me too. I'll play," Wheezy added. "The festival got my motor running. Strike while my fingers are hot."

"No. I'm doing this alone." Jon shook his head with finality. "I'm *not* putting any of you in harm's way."

"Uh-uh. We're playing the gig, right, Legs?"

"If you say so." Legs smiled with a plan on his face. "We do like Thelma and the Wheez gettin' that harmonica back."

Jon chuckled. "None of you are getting a gun. And you're certainly not going over a cliff for that harmonica, Legs."

"I know I'm not! You do the driving, G-man."

"This is perfect, Jon!" Jean stood and smacked her hands together. "Legs and Wheezy can play at the party and create a distraction. When these guys show up, Forrester won't be able to resist giving Legs the harmonica. Nobody has to 'get' anything. Kip will hand it over."

"Road trip!" Wheezy shouted.

"Whoa! Guys! All of you are not going with me."

"Yes, we are."

"What about Not Fade Away?" Jon rubbed his face. He had no hope of getting out of this.

Jean turned to Spence. "Can Bill handle the store alone for one day?"

"Saturday will be busy," Spence said. "Maybe I'll call Dillon to cover for me."

"Perfect! He loves being at the store. We should be home in time to feed Mycroft. It'll be late, but he'll be fine."

Spence bolted to the kitchen and picked up the phone. Jon followed him in the hope that he'd be the voice of reason.

"I can't guarantee the schedule," Jon hedged. "I could be with Forrester and Hughes for hours."

"If you get hung up, we'll just rent a car to come back," Spence countered. "Hey, Jean, did you check the messages?"

"Not yet," she called back.

"There are three here from this morning."

As Jean joined them, Spence pressed the speaker button and retrieved the messages. The first two were from Dan Brick, insisting they call to set up a meeting. Jon rolled his eyes and waved his hand to dismiss them. On the third, Anhur's voice made all three of them freeze. Jean stared at Spence with a pained expression.

"Now what do we do?"

"Erase that message," Jon said, "and be in my car on Saturday morning. We need to get ourselves out of town." Jon wiped his face and rubbed the top of his crew cut. "I can't go back into the office before we leave for Seattle."

"Should we pick up Anhur at the Hyatt and get him out of town too?" Jean asked.

"No, let him deal with Brick. He's a smart man. If Anhur tells him the truth, Brick will either freak out or keep his mouth shut like I did. He's obviously already talked with Brick."

"We'll need to face this at some point," Jean said, turning to Spence. "What do you think?"

"No desire to talk to Brick right now. I'm fine with trusting Anhur to handle him until after Saturday."

"We *will* deal with this," Jon said, "but not until I have Forrester and Hughes in custody." He turned and stepped back to the living room. With his hands on his hips, Jon stood and studied Legs and Wheezy. "Don't you guys have to go home soon?"

"Home to what? The action is right here," Wheezy said.

Legs nodded as he inspected the back cover of *I Am the Blues* by Willie Dixon from 1970. "Did some-a these with Muddy. Uh-huh." He handed Wheezy the album. "Put this on the spinner. 'Hoochie Coochie Man.'"

Wheezy spread his arms at Jon. "We don't have to leave until Jean and Spence kick us out. Until then, this is a happenin'!" Wheezy waved Willie Dixon's black-and-white image at Jon and opened his mouth in a silent laugh.

"Something's going to happen all right." Jon rubbed his forehead. "Be ready to leave at ten o'clock on Saturday morning. I must be crazy."

CHAPTER 15

Rational Answers

Dan Brick ushered Anhur Kumar into his office on Friday morning. Anhur thought the man's jaw was set too tight for productive discussion. Taking a seat in front of the agent's desk, Anhur waited for Brick to calm down. His gaze followed the man's frustration around the office.

"I can't reach the Collinses," Brick griped. "Jon's not answering his phone either." Too agitated to sit, Dan paced in front of the window. Anhur's gaze followed him like it would a quiet tennis match on sprouting turf.

"They are quite busy," Anhur suggested. Finding the histrionics less than enlightening, he attempted to understand the man through personal effects in his office. There were none. Unusual for both the desk and credenza to be void of even one personal photo, not even a diploma of pride on the wall. More than he revealed lurked beneath the man's shell. Anhur was beginning to think of Agent Brick as a personal project—a challenge to be conquered.

"And Jon wasn't in the office yesterday, or this morning either. I even went to the Collinses' house. No one answered." Dan stopped and pointed to him. "Did you tip them off?"

Crossing his leg and brushing the knee of his bespoke suit, Anhur attempted to calm the atmosphere.

"Shall we continue our discussion? We may not need for any of them to be here."

"I don't know. Let me think." Dan sat and smacked the desk.

"Sit. Please, Agent Brick. There is still much you need to under-stand."

The charged atmosphere stilled as he followed the instruction. The agent pressed on his eyebrows. Anhur imagined they were stuck on with adhesive like false eyelashes. *Blink and you shall see.*

"What? You're staring at me. Are you trying to hypnotize me or something"

Anhur decided to try a new direction.

"Do you share your life with a partner, Agent Brick? Someone you care very much for?"

Brick raised his eyes, confused by the question. "No." He paused and glanced to the window. He sighed. "Well, almost…once. She called off the wedding. For the best. Why?"

"You cannot hope to understand the forces at work here unless you embrace the ability to love someone beyond yourself, more than yourself." Anhur ran his hand over the leather pouch in his lap. Without looking up, he said, "Since you didn't ask, I care for this fabric beyond anything, or anyone, in my life. This passion is mis-placed, I'm sorry to say. I am filled with many regrets in pursuit of a career. Until the Collinses brought this to me, I had no idea—no *concept*—of the meaning of a beating heart."

"What the hell is that supposed to mean?"

"You must come out of your uncomfortable place of order and rigidity. Put aside conventions."

"There's a rational answer to everything. But so far, none of this makes any sense."

"Understanding requires an expansion of the term *rational*, my friend. Some elements of life cannot be explained but only em-braced."

"Did the Collinses kill Raleigh Coulter with that fabric in your lap?" Brick snapped, changing the subject. "I'm convinced Jon Segert was involved."

"Nonsense. Innocent witnesses. However, I can attest to what Jean and Spencer experienced in Cairo after the death of the man in London."

Brick stared at him in defiance. Anhur pondered the information he'd withheld from their earlier conversation.

"I need *proof*. You haven't told me everything, Mr. Kumar."

"You are correct."

"I hope you have better answers than the ones you gave me at the hotel."

Anhur set the pouch with the fabric on Brick's desk and reached in his pocket. He pulled out the flash drive.

"What's that?"

"This is a recording of the transformation the Collinses initiated in my office at the museum in Cairo. The actual process of making Mary Coulter immortal."

The agent studied the device with a conflicted mixture of discovery and skepticism on his face. The emotions turned to temptation and finally hunger. But Anhur didn't hand it over right away.

"I am the only one who has viewed this event," he continued, "not even members of the museum's board. What you see will impress upon you the importance of keeping this fabric protected."

Dan held out his hand. "Give it here."

Anhur closed his eyes and handed him the drive. *No reverse of course.*

The small device slipped into the side of Brick's computer. He clicked the mouse. A windowed file appeared with an arrow to start the video. Dan increased the volume on the speakers.

Anhur leaned forward to narrate. Recorded from a camera in the ceiling, the opening black-and-white image showed the fabric displayed on a long, highly polished conference table. The birds were clearly visible. The Collinses stood in front of them, nervous and shifting from foot to foot.

Spence, do you want to do it, or should I?

Let's do it together.

"Here the process starts when the hands are placed on the fabric," Anhur said.

"Does it happen any time you do that?"

"No. The Collinses have just received word that Mary Coulter suffered a catastrophic stroke. They initiated the process specifically for Mrs. Coulter in the event she did not recover."

"Uh-huh."

From the overhead view, Jean placed her hands on two of the birds. Spencer did the same. Their fingers appeared to heave from the fabric's surface. The Collinses' faces couldn't be seen, but the birds in the cloth began to fade. They disappeared. In the video, Anhur stood next to the back wall of his office, wiping his face on the sleeve of his shirt. All three of them turned their heads to something out of view.

"What are the three of you staring at, Mr. Kumar?" Dan tapped the bottom of his screen at the edge of the frozen picture.

Anhur closed his eyes, recalling every detail beyond the camera. He forced himself to open them.

"The phoenixes, Mr. Brick," he whispered. "The phoenixes emerged from the fabric and waited for us on the balcony rail outside of my office. If you look closely, you will find the fabric empty."

Brick furrowed his brow and turned back to the computer screen. He clicked the mouse to resume watching the video.

The Collinses and Anhur ran out of view of the recording. The fabric was left unattended on the conference table. Only the faintest of swirled lines remained behind.

"You went outside?" Brick paused the video.

"Yes, we followed their flight. Magnificent sight. You cannot appreciate their size. I could have reached out and touched them. Out of respect I did not." Anhur pointed. His thick gold ring with an etched scarab, a diamond mounted on its back, flashed in the light. "Continue, please."

Brick clicked the mouse. In the image, Jean grasped Spence's arm as they reappeared in the office.

We have to go! They'll return to the fabric once Mary completes the process...if we can complete the process. Anhur, we need to be on the next flight back to America!

"From this point forward, I arranged for the Collinses to return to Portland in order to give Mary Coulter immortality."

As Dan stared at Anhur, a riot of emotions washed over his face. He turned back to the screen with the frozen image of where the video ended.

"How...did that...kill Raleigh Coulter?" he stuttered, shaking his finger at the leather pouch. Brick obviously couldn't rationalize what he'd witnessed on the recording.

"When threatened, the phoenixes take on a completely different form. They are not birds, Mr. Brick; they are manifestations of Egyptian gods. Raleigh Coulter precipitated the emergence of Horus—in the body of a hawk—when he stole the fabric from Jean in London. Horus is protective, but malevolent when his charge is threatened."

"Do you have video of that too?"

"I myself have not observed that particular transformation. Only the Collineses and Jon Segert can describe the events that took place."

Brick copied the recording to his hard drive and pulled out the device. He turned it over in his fingers as if it too might transform. He hesitated and then released it back into the custody of Anhur's hand.

"I can't put this in front of a court, or even the chief," he whispered, wiping his forehead. "They'll think I'm nuts."

"I believe your dilemma is the same moral complication Agent Segert experienced. Many implications."

"Stay here. I'll be right back."

Brick marched to Jenny Kowalski's cubicle. She swiveled from her computer to face him and took a sip of a fruit smoothie. With the straw in her mouth, she threw him an amused gaze.

"Where's Jon?" he demanded.

"He's on assignment. Hasn't been in here since Wednesday night." Jenny shrugged. "Go ask the chief."

A hot flush filled his face. He pounded down the hall to the corner office. He stood in the doorway and knocked on the open door.

"What?" the chief snapped without raising his eyes.

"Where's Segert? I need to talk to him."

"I'm not his nanny. He's on a case. Leave him alone."

"I…uh…got the fabric back from Egypt. Anhur Kumar's in my office now."

"Well, goody for you, Brick. If I had wanted Segert to spend any more time on the Coulter investigation, he'd still be working it. I turned the case over to you to free him up. He's on to something with this insider trading crap. I take this seriously. I owned Enron stock."

"He's holding crucial details about Coulter…the way he died. Weird information about the hawk in Raleigh's taxi. Jon's hiding from me."

"What did he do? Take a walk like an Egyptian?" The chief's belly bobbed under his stiff white shirt.

"This is serious, Chief! Another piece to all this has come to light, and I think that piece is connected to Dromov too. Remember how he said a hawk bit his arm?"

"I'm gonna bite your arm if you don't leave my office. You want to get to the bottom of it, then interrogate the claw he's got." The chair squealed as the chief rocked with his fingers laced. "Could do an autopsy on a gnat, the damned thing's so sharp. Besides, you'll have to wait for him to get back from Seattle."

"What's he doing in Seattle?"

"Unlike you, he did real investigative work to solve his case. Jon's about to take down Forrester and Hughes. Kip and his snitch are going to jail thanks to that weasel, Nash Winthrop. Brilliant." He nodded his head like he'd already sold the rights for a movie deal.

"Where's Segert now?"

"Hell if I know. James Bond is probably off renting a tuxedo for the swanky party at Forrester's house tomorrow night. Sounds like a fun takedown."

"I just watched a video of the Collinses in Cairo."

"And...?"

"Well...those two are in cahoots with Segert and Kumar and into some weird stuff."

"What kind of stuff?"

"Stuff."

"Will you let go of this damned vendetta of yours, Brick?" The chief peered over his cheap drugstore cheaters. "I mean it. This is not how things get done around here."

"I'm taking Kumar to Seattle."

"You'll do no such thing. Not on my dime, you won't."

"Damned if I'm not!" Dan turned and stomped back to his office.

"Brick!"

CHAPTER 16

Road Trip

"Everybody in and buckled up?" Jean asked after they'd all piled into the black Crown Victoria on Saturday morning. Spence sat in front with Jon; she settled in back with Wheezy and Legs. Wheezy dangled his shoes over the hump in the middle, looking more like a ventriloquist's mouthpiece than a brilliant piano player. "Can you see, Wheezy?"

"Get you one of them booster seats the little kids use at the drive-in," Legs said, pointing his long thumb at Wheezy.

"Yeah, yeah. Ha-ha. The G-man up there almost had to rent a stretch limo to fit you," Wheezy snapped back.

"Got enough room, Legs?" Spence glided the seat forward with an electric whir, stopping when the mechanism reached its limit.

"Pay no mind. Pay no mind. I'm good. Used to eatin' my knees."

"So, G-man, how much does this bucket of bolts cost us hardworking taxpayers, anyway?" Wheezy laughed.

"Do I have to endure this for the next three hours, Beevers? Are you going to bust my chops all the way to Seattle?" Jon glanced into the rearview mirror and grimaced.

"Depends. If we get to stop for lunch—maybe a juicy steak—I'll cut you a break."

"I might go for one of those, yes, I could," Legs added, elbowing Wheezy. "And runny eggs."

"All right—enough." Jon put the car into drive. He rolled down the window. The thin flap of wispy hair on Wheezy's head stood up straight.

"Put some glass in the hole," Wheezy shouted. "Or Jean needs to give me a squirt of her girly goo to hold down my 'do." He licked his fingers and smoothed the tendril over his otherwise bald head.

"Cut that thing off, Wheez. Do like mine." Legs spit in his hand and rubbed the top of his shiny scalp. Spence wiped his eyes, laughing as Legs actually made his head squeak.

Jon sighed and hit the switch on the window and turned on the air conditioner.

"In case you get hungry, Wheezy, I brought some trail mix and roasted almonds, no salt," Spence said, turning from the front seat.

"I'm not eatin' the stuff. Squirrel food. Forget about it."

"Bear cubs eat that," Legs added. "Taste like dirt. Too much roughy. Give you some scratch."

"Fine, you guys. More for me." Spence poured a handful of nuts and raisins in his mouth.

As the group settled in for their trek up Interstate 5, Jean wanted to use the trip to learn about Legs's and Wheezy's histories. They'd jumped into the craziness of the concert event and the opening of the store without having spent quality time with the fellas.

"So, Legs? How did you and Wheezy meet?" Jean asked. Spence turned with his arm over the seat to hear the story too. Judging by the number of times Jean saw Jon glance in the rearview mirror, back at her and the musicians, he was dividing his attention between the road and the stories.

"Playin' my horn in a club in Chicago in '48. Wheez in the crowd, jus' a kid in college. So, that night my piano man had a little bit too much imbibilation, if you know what I mean."

"Passed out cold was more like it! Dead-dog drunk," Wheezy interjected, raising his hands in exasperation.

"You done pokin' in my story? Not enough air in this car with you pushin' it around too."

Sweeping his hand, Wheezy motioned for Legs to keep going.

"Well, all a sudden the bench be empty. Piano man was laid out on the floor. I put down my horn and pull him by his feet to git 'im off the stage. Next thing I know, this white kid be sittin' at the keys. Was Franklin Beevers. Now you talk, Wheez."

"Franklin?" Spence said, laughing. Jean couldn't hold back a giggle. Jon pressed his lips together.

"Yeah…" Wheezy sighed. "What else was a short, fat, rich kid to do with a name like Franklin, except study music at Oberlin?" He crossed his arms. "*Really*, parents can be so cruel."

"Don't forget you had on big magnifyin' glasses too. Pull the wings off a no-see-um with those things." Legs chuckled and widened his eyes with his thumbs and forefingers. Wheezy pretended to ignore him.

"I was a classical pianist. Me and jazz became one in that club. The music got inside me and came out through my fingers. I'd go into dozens of clubs to hear the greats play back in the late forties. When that guy passed out, I jumped on the stage, started playing. All she wrote. I quit school the same year. My parents were ready to disown me. Back then, the lines of propriety were pretty strict. Jazz was on the wrong side of it in my snooty family. They had plans for me to get my master's at Juilliard after Oberlin. Grand delusions of me playing on the concert stage to impress their fancy friends."

"Impressive pedigree for a jazz musician," Jean said.

"Rachmaninoff to riffin'. Right, Legs?" Wheezy laughed in windy silence.

"Liszt to licks…uh-huh. Now those are some braggin' rights. Me and Wheez play together for the next thirty years. Been through a lot." Legs gazed out the window as if *a lot* were scrolling by in the blur of the trees. "Last time in Portland was back in '49, downtown in McElroy's Ballroom. Bet they tore it down." Legs rubbed the gray stubble on his chin.

"Yeah, they did," Spence added. "It's the Portland Building now."

A pall settled over the car. The mention of tearing down music venues seemed to crumble Legs's mood into the rubble. It must have felt like a habitat for an endangered musical species had been sold and bulldozed. Jean switched gears.

"Legs? When we visited you in DC, the shelf over the television had a picture of a woman, right next to Ella Fitzgerald's. Was she your wife?" Fortunately, the warm magic Jean had felt that afternoon at Legs's house seemed to connect with that photo too, as Legs's expression, though wistful, was positive.

"Rose," Legs said in a faraway voice. He remained quiet after saying her name. His ebony eyes flickered with a watery reflection of sunlight.

"Rosey Rosey, Rosey," Wheezy cooed, resting his head back on the seat. He reached to graze his fingers over the fabric roof line, not quite able to touch the fuzz. "An angel. I told Legs if he didn't marry her, I would." He glanced at Jean, dipping his glasses to peer above them. "Legs dragged his feet. Thought he'd be tied down. Can you believe that? Well, if not having a Rosey in your life is freedom, then send me to *jail*." Wheezy turned to Legs. "How long were you—"

"Thirty-nine wonderful years. You were right, you know, to say I'd be a crazy fool not to get hitched. Lucky man, yes, I was. She gave me two fine sons."

Those must be the young men in the Navy uniforms in the photos at Legs's house, Jean decided.

"Lost Rose in '89, I did," Legs continued. "Had a bad heart and mine broke too. I miss her, I sure do."

Jean's eyes misted, not so much from the words themselves but in the way Legs said them. He'd lost more than a spouse; he'd lost the love of his life. She glanced at Spence, and then at Jon in the rearview mirror. He had a thoughtful gaze, probably thinking about Meg, his wife.

"She was a helluva cook too," Wheezy added. "I had a hard butt before Rosey started feeding me. I can still taste those green beans she used to make with onions and little bits of ham. Mmmm-mmm."

"Never go hungry at my house," Legs said. "Nothin' better than comin' home from the road to Rosey's cookin'."

"What about you, Wheezy?" Spence asked. "Did you have anyone special in your life?"

Wheezy wrinkled his nose. "Not even close. I'm a vicarious observer of the relationships of others. Just me and my Bösendorfer."

"But you're so lovable," Jean added and wrapped her arm around his.

"You're taken, Jean."

"Legs? Were your sons in the military? In their pictures, they look like twins in their uniforms," Spence said.

"Andrew and Alton. Doubled up, they were. Good as gold…good boys. Jus' twenty when they got called up for 'Nam. Lost 'em both one month apart…one month." Legs's voice trailed off, reliving the nightmare of the news as if he'd received the calls only yesterday.

"Back in '67, the tour from hell." Wheezy's usually buoyant cheeks seemed to sag. "Hell on the road and in the war. We played with Louis Armstrong toward the end of his career. Legs had just met back up with the band after the first funeral when the second call came from Rosey about Alton. Louis was torn up too. He always took good care of you, Legs. He gave you his handkerchief after you hung up that phone backstage. May not sound like much, but what would be enough in the face of such news? There were a lot of tears that day."

Jean rubbed her brow. *So that's how he got Louis Armstrong's handkerchief.* She remembered admiring it in the glass cabinet in Legs's living room. At the time, she'd thought it was given to Legs in celebration of a successful gig or maybe in response to an inspired performance. She knew it was special but never guessed the embroidered piece of cloth with Louis's initials carried so much personal significance.

The hum of the car's engine was the only sound for a few minutes.

Wheezy shifted in his seat. "C'mon guys. This is no time to be maudlin." Wheezy slapped his knees. "What about you, G-man? You're awfully quiet. How'd you get to be a secret agent man?"

Jean tapped Jon's shoulder with her forefinger. "Yeah, you never told us how you got into the FBI."

"I'm nothing special. I like to chase bad guys, listen to the Rolling Stones, and watch old reruns of *Columbo*."

"That must be why you always save the best bad-guy lines for when you're walking out the door," Jean quipped. She turned to Wheezy and whispered, "He's a great interrogator."

"Fifteen years with the FBI now. Before that, I was a cop. When I unraveled an identity theft ring, the agents I worked with recruited me. Don't ever throw out any papers without shredding them first."

"What about the *love* department?" Wheezy asked.

"I've got a great wife, Meg, who does fund-raising for animal charities. My daughter, Amy, is in college. I adore her. End of story."

"Ahem…excuse me, Jon, not entirely the whole story."

"Then…on a flight to London I met these two on a case related to the one I'm working now." Jon smirked at Jean's reflected gaze. "Jean and Spence changed my life in many ways."

"We stick our noses into Jon's cases. We learned about you, Legs, when we got involved in the Dromov mess with a painting of ours. Every little connection leads to something fantastic. We're Jon's magic bullets."

"Jean…" Spence warned.

"No, she's right. *The Dancing Boy* will do a lot of good when it's sold."

"Must-a been some painting," Legs interjected. "Like the one your cat go in?"

Jon shot a quizzical look at Spence.

"Yeah, we had to tell them about what happened at the festival," Spence said and shrugged. "Couldn't come up with a more rational explanation."

Jean turned to the window. "Yes, quite special, Legs. Filled with magic."

"Going to be sold soon, though," Jon continued. "Hanging in my office until then."

"When?" Wheezy straightened in his seat.

"In a month or so. We need to find the right buyer. All the proceeds will be given to Dromov's victims…per Jean and Spence's instructions."

"Good people. Yes, you are." Legs patted Spence's shoulder.

"I'm hungry," Wheezy announced.

"If there's a drain hole close too, I think it has my name on it."

"Okay, but we're not far away. We're coming up on Puyallup, near Sea-Tac Airport. We'll stop there." Jon switched lanes to exit the freeway.

"Puyallup? What kind of town is that? Sounds like something I had removed last year." Wheezy made an *O* of his mouth and squinted his eyes.

"Got a 'scopy too, not so long ago." Legs nodded in sympathy. "Didn't find nothin'. Clean as a whistle, yes, I was."

"You ever had that done G-man? You look old." Wheezy clearly enjoyed getting a rise out of Jon.

"Nooo…I haven't had one. Meg keeps bugging me, though." Jon's voice had a hint of embarrassment, or maybe denial that he'd crossed the fifty-yard line.

"I hated drinking all the stuff the night before." Jean wrinkled her nose.

"You said it made you feel skinny," Spence countered. Jon smirked and shook his head.

"Me too." Wheezy thumped his stomach, round like a ripe melon. "I could practically see my backbone through my belly button. Speaking of which, you said we were going to stop for steak." He pointed and elbowed Jean. "Hey! A sign for Polyps."

"Puyallup," Jon corrected. "Enough out of you, Beevers."

Legs slapped his knees, turning the rhythm of his words into a riff. "Gettin' Muddy's harmonica back…"

"Gettin' Forrester behind bars," Jon added, thumping the steering wheel in syncopation against Legs's beat.

"Gettin the bad guys," Spence said in a singsong and drummed the dashboard.

"Gettin' a steak, so Legs can go to the bathroom," Wheezy sang, clicking his wingtips.

Everyone started laughing. Wheezy wheezed.

CHAPTER 17

Forrester for the Trees

They'd found the right place. Jon slowed the Crown Victoria at the top of the hill. In this exclusive neighborhood, distinctive custom homes on wooded lots loomed over downtown Seattle. Peeks of twinkle lights reminded him of the elevation. Kip Forrester's house remained hidden behind a thick stand of old-growth cedar trees illuminated with floodlights mounted high in the branches; the effect was eerie and expensive. A pair of flaming tiki light poles flanked the gaping wrought-iron gates. The onset of dusk had triggered the domed ground lights that dotted the edge of the circular driveway snaking through the private woods.

"I can't see the house with all the trees," Jean whispered. "Get closer."

"We're not on a home tour, Jean," Spence chided.

"Open for business, G-man," Wheezy said. "Let's go in and get liquored up."

"Things might start makin' some sense," Legs said.

Legs went quiet, taking in the scene. Jon figured his wheels were spinning inside his calm exterior.

"Too early." Jon inspected the layout of the grounds, calculating their next move. "We'll wait down here until somebody else pulls in. I still haven't figured out how to get you guys inside."

Jon pulled to the curb, shut off his headlights, and kept the engine idling. He wanted to wait for somebody to arrive so he could follow up the driveway without being seen.

"So what's the plan again?" Jean asked.

"We have three goals. I'm not sure of the best way to do this, but first we need to get the boys playing with the band. Trust me; Kip will give Legs the harmonica. He won't be able to resist."

"Got it. I'll tear the place up." Wheezy thumped the front seat.

"No doubt." Jean patted his leg. "Next?"

"Second, I need to wait for Braxton Hughes to arrive. Then I'll go inside. And third, I'll take Forrester and Hughes aside after the music starts. We'll have a talk."

"What about Spence and me?" Jean leaned forward with her hands on Jon's headrest.

"Stay in the car and keep an eye out. I'll be calling for backup. Seattle police are on standby."

Jean's shoulders slumped. "But I'm all dressed up. I thought we were supposed to be guests." The sparkly beads on the front of her black sweater reflected the light from the house.

"Honey, we'll be his eyes outside. Don't get your nose out of joint." Spence gave his head a slight shake and put his fingers to his lips.

"You'll be the prettiest one in a Crown Vic," Jon quipped. "Shhh…here comes somebody."

The high beams from a tall truck crested the hill and turned in front of them through the gates. *A-1 Rentals* was written on the side. The light snaked through the trees. He started up the drive behind the truck.

Lights flickered through the branches as the Crown Victoria inched toward their source. Out of the clearing, the modern structure seemed to jump off the pages of *Architectural Digest*. The truck stopped at the entrance. Jon pulled into a wooded area far enough away that they would be unseen by the casual observer at the house but near enough that they'd still have a view of the front door.

"Wow!" Spence gawked at the house. The two-story structure

was built using mixed textures of cedar, glass, cantilevered steel, and stacked river rock. The interior illumination made the structure appear ready for a photo shoot. The architecturally compatible design blended with the natural surroundings.

"We're not house hunting, remember?" Jean poked Spence's shoulder. "Looks like that cool house in *North by Northwest*. You know, the one Cary Grant sneaks into to save Eva Marie Saint on Mount Rushmore?"

"Dirty money," Jon said, studying the outside details and plotting the home's layout inside. "He won't be living here for long."

The doors on back of the rental truck swung open, revealing sound equipment and hard-sided cases on wheels. Four men—two white, two black—in cream tuxedos jumped out and carried their instruments into the house. Two roadies hoisted a drum kit.

"Where's the piano?" Wheezy asked.

"Probably already inside. I'm sure he owns one—a famous one. People should start arriving in about twenty minutes." Jon kept his gaze focused on the front door. "There's Kip. He looks pissed." He cracked the window to listen.

"Where have you guys been? I told you to be here an hour ago!" Kip shouted. "My guests will be coming up the drive any minute. You'll still be setting up!" He resembled a member of an eighties band in his off-white suit, shiny purple shirt, and thin black tie. Even his hairstyle was a rocker knockoff. "Move this truck! The valet needs to get to the cars." He stormed back inside the house.

"Why am I hearing the theme song of *Miami Vice*?" Spence quipped. "What a tool."

"I'm sure he thinks his outfit is cool. Probably has glitter in his perm," Jean added.

"Muddy be rollin' over in his grave knowin' a guy like that got his harp." Legs rested his head in his hand.

"Forget him. Check out the equipment being unloaded." Wheezy gawked through the windshield. "Top of the line."

The roadies set more large cases on the driveway. The truck

pulled away to a graveled side area on the opposite side of the house. Jon watched one of the workers open a wheeled case and lift out an amplifier. He hefted it to the door and disappeared.

"The case!" Jean blurted out. "That's how Wheezy can get in! Legs can roll him."

Everyone in the car turned and stared at her.

"Could work," Spence said in the silence. "Once they're in, it'll be hard to roust them out. I'll attest to that." He laughed. "No offense, guys."

"You serious?" Jon said and chuckled. "Will you fit in that, Wheezy?"

The four of them studied the empty case in the driveway, assessing its size against Wheezy's girth. If he curled up, he could be shoved in.

"Yeah, roll Wheezy in like a piece of equipment," Jean said. "Legs can be one of the roadies—a really tall one."

"Wait, wait. Let's think about this." Jon noodled the plan. If he had any sanity at all, he'd screech the brakes on this—pronto.

"Wheez?" Legs scratched his chin. "You wanna be a speaker for a spell? You get in. I'll push."

"I'm not a rescue sea lion, Legs." Wheezy grimaced.

"No, you ain't got a tail like one, but the rest of you 'bout right. Nobody pay any mind to me." Legs pulled the handle on the door and extended one long leg outside. "Let's get you in 'fore somebody come back out. Stop this sittin' around. Bad for the blood."

Jean nudged Wheezy's knee. "Quick! Go while nobody's up there."

"I bet the food's catered. A little nosh sounds good." Wheezy scooted across the seat and popped out next to Legs. He brushed his suit jacket and flexed his knees. "Throw me a fish, Big Guy."

Legs leaned down and said, "Catch you inside, G-man." He pressed the car door until it latched with a quiet click.

They'd already started up the driveway before Jon could protest.

"Wait! Guys!" Jon leaned his head in his hand. "I don't know about this."

"They'll be fine," Jean assured.

"There's no way I'm letting them go up there alone. Stay here." Jon opened the car door.

Legs trekked up the driveway toward the speaker case. His nonchalant gait exuded confidence. Behind him, wingtips clacked to catch up. Jon followed. Legs slipped his hands under Wheezy's armpits. He grunted and turned to Jon.

"Liftin' him be a challenge," Legs said. "Thought I could do it, but I got a 'roid with Wheezy's name on it."

"Here. Let me do this." Jon took his place and braced himself for the lift.

"Be gentle, G-man. I'm light as a feather." Wheezy stuck out his arms.

Jon's face turned purple as he hoisted Wheezy into the speaker case. One of his hard-soled shoes caught on the side, forcing Wheezy to straddle the metal-rimmed edge.

"Watch it! Up! Up! You're slicing my nuts into sushi!" Wheezy's mouth made a large *O* as he squinted his eyes.

"Sorry, Wheezy," Jon said, wincing at the more-than-awkward position.

"You made-a lead," Legs chided, swishing his long arm. "Quit eatin' all that cheese."

"Lift me. Quick!"

"That has got to hurt," Legs said.

"Let's try this again." Jon pulled up Wheezy, clattering his shoes on the rim. After giving Wheezy a serious wedgie, Jon lowered him inside.

Legs closed the lid. He didn't latch the buckles. Better source of air.

"Get moving! My teeth are popping out. I feel like a marshmallow in a piggy bank," Wheezy griped, sounding as though he were talking from under a blanket.

"Quit your fussin'. Here we go." Legs grabbed the handle. "You get the other side Fed-man."

Legs and Jon rolled the box up the sidewalk toward the front door. Legs waved at one of the valets on his way back to his station.

"How you doin'?" he said above the rattle of the latches. "Playin' tonight. Settin' up. My roadie here helpin'. Give a hand to my man and lift this case up." Legs stood back and directed traffic.

"Sure." The young man rolled up the sleeves of his white shirt and grasped the handle of the case. He lifted the wheels to the first step. "What do you have in here, a speaker from 1962?"

"He's an old one but still plays good." Legs smiled as he let the two younger men do the heavy work. Jon's eyes bulged at the weight.

Ba-bang!

"Careful now. Got some delicate parts." Legs remained cool and collected. Jon, not so much.

"I'm trying," the valet groaned and blew out a breath.

"Almost…to the…top step," Jon groaned.

A grunt rumbled under the lid. Legs smiled as if he'd released the noise and nodded for Jon to keep moving forward. Jon smirked and did one final lift.

Ba-bang!

"'Preciate the help. Go on back to your valetin'." Legs's gaze followed the valet down the sidewalk. He turned back to Jon. "You okay, Fed-man?"

"What about me?" Wheezy shouted from inside the case.

"Quit your bitchin'," Legs ordered, stooping to speak directly to the lid.

"Yeah, but goddamn—he's heavy." Jon rubbed his hands. "Can you take him from here, Legs?"

"Smooth as a baby's bottom." Legs smiled wide. "You go on back to the car."

Legs waited for Jon to clear the sidewalk and leaned down to the buckles. "All right, Wheez?"

"I'm alive, if that's what you mean. Stinks it here. Smells like gym socks."

"That you?"

"Not laughing."

Legs glided the case into the entryway. The curved staircase and oversize art made him somewhat dizzy. The open layout of the downstairs and expensive modern furniture was impressive.

"Oooo-eeee. Some digs."

"What? I wanna see." Wheezy started to pop the top, but Legs pressed on the lid.

"Wait here, Wheez. I gotta check on where they settin' up the band."

"Where the hell am I gonna go?"

"You might do like them dogs with no legs in those wheelie carts. Don't be rollin' around, now."

Stretching to his full height, Legs took long, quiet steps down the hall toward the back of the house. The thrum of instruments being tuned led him to two sets of double French doors that opened to an expansive patio. One of the musicians practiced a few riffs for tuning, while another tested the sound level of a white baby grand piano. He turned and headed back to the front entryway to get Wheezy. As Legs approached the staircase, he froze. A vision of cream, purple, and black stood at the bottom of the stairs.

"Who are you?" Kip asked.

"Harmonica player. Jus' settin' up." Legs wiped his hand over the top of his bald head, all the while keeping an eye on the speaker case. His eyes widened when Wheezy lifted the lid a couple of inches.

"I told you guys to go through the back. My guests will be here any—" Kip stopped. His face changed into a broad smile. "Wait a minute. I know you. You're Legs Flanders!"

"The same," Legs said, nodding. "Fancy digs."

"Kip Forrester, Mr. Flanders." He pumped Legs's hand. "This is a surprise. What are you doing here?"

"Heard you had my harmonica and was holdin' a big gig tonight.

I happen to be in tree country, so I said to myself, 'I think I want to play that harp one more time.'"

"Yeah…" Kip shook his finger. "You were down in Portland last weekend. Sorry I didn't make it; I heard you and Wheezy did quite a show." His face brightened as if he had a brilliant idea. "But, hey, how about a private concert?"

"Snappin' alligators couldn't hold me back. Brought my friend Wheezy too."

"Wheezy Beevers? I'll be damned! C'mon, let me introduce you to some people. I have a photographer outside. Let's have a picture together with the harmonica. This isn't going to be just any party; you guys will *be* the party. Where's Wheezy? I'd love to meet him."

"Oh, he'll be rollin' in here by the by." Legs glanced over his shoulder as Kip reached up and gave him a friendly slap on the back. "Somethin' good cookin' in the kitchen. Mmm-mmm."

"Grab a plate and help yourself. Roasted fresh salmon. They're just pouring the champagne."

Wheezy raised the lid on the case about three inches, peering out like an infuriated clam.

CHAPTER 18

Pass the Champagne

Shiny sports cars streamed up the driveway, an opulent convoy. The coordinated timing indicated a pre-party might have taken place. Keys were handed over to the valet. Their owners were dressed to impress. A red carpet seemed more appropriate than a concrete sidewalk for the hundred or so guests.

Jean leaned toward Jon's shoulder.

"What are we waiting for? I'm worried about Legs and Wheezy being inside the house all by themselves."

"Be patient," Jon instructed. "We're not going to storm the place. Got to play this cool. I'm trying to spot Hughes."

"What's he look like?" Spence asked.

"Bald, tall, glasses, about fifty-five. Think Lumpy's father on *Leave It to Beaver*." Jon smirked and scratched his upper lip. "Now comes the chess game. Once the boys start playing, the crowd will be occupied. Listen for the piano."

Spence whirred down the window six inches.

"You have the talon?" Jean whispered.

"I do."

"Can I hold it—just for a minute?" Jean opened her palm over the front seat.

Jon reached in his pocket and pulled out the three-inch curved claw and held it up to the reflected lights from the house. The silhouette's lethal shadow narrowed to a needle's tip.

"Careful."

Jean ran her finger along the edge and flicked the point with her fingernail. Spence held up his hand to stop her.

"Horus likes us. He won't do anything." She handed the talon back to Jon. Headlights illuminated the car through the back window. Jean turned and sucked in a breath. The tightness in her chest reminded her to exhale. A car pulled up behind them, so close the headlights disappeared into the Crown Victoria's bumper.

The face was only a shadow, but Jean recognized the square-jawed outline in the driver's seat. "That's Brick!"

"Brick," Jon echoed in a whisper. He narrowed his eyes in the rearview mirror at what was surely a twin Crown Victoria.

"What the hell is he doing here?" Spence smacked his knee.

"Somebody's with him," Jean added. "I think it's Anhur!" She pulled the handle on the door.

"Stop. Don't move!" Jon ordered. "We can't draw attention to ourselves."

Dan Brick stepped out, adjusted the waist of his slacks, and sauntered toward Jon's window. He tapped the glass with his knuckles.

Jon hit the switch but lowered the window only halfway. "Why are you here? I'm about to wrap this up."

"I have my own investigation going, Segert. And you're at the center of the action. I've seen some things that'll curl your grandmother's hair."

"Sorry you wasted a trip. Go back to Portland."

"We're doing this now. Get out of the car. All of you."

"No. Not happening. We're waiting for the music to start. Then we're going in the house."

Brick whirled his hand, signaling for Anhur to join him. He opened the back door and motioned for Jean to move over to the other window. Her gaze followed Anhur as he approached with something in his hands. Brick waited for Anhur to slide into the middle, and then ducked in behind him.

"You are here! Oh my God!" Jean exclaimed.

Sliding in beside her with a leather-wrapped bundle tucked under his arm, Anhur gave her a warm embrace. He reached over and shook Spence's hand. "We finally meet again. I do wish under better circumstances."

Brick frowned and addressed Jon. "Anhur filled me in on that piece of cloth. A bunch of hocus-pocus. All three of you are using it as a cover for God knows what."

"The fabric's with you?" Jean said, nearly forgetting their true mission. "Can I see it?"

"Not here. Not now, Jean." The increased edge in Jon's voice dampened the reunion.

Anhur patted the pouch. "In due time."

Jon narrowed his eyes. "How much did you fill him in on, Mr. Kumar?"

"Nearly all, with the exception of your experience, Mr. Segert. I cannot speak for you. I apologize, but—"

"No, no, the truth would come out eventually. Better sooner than later, I guess." Jon turned to Brick. "Your timing stinks. Put all of this aside and help me for once."

Brick leaned back in the seat. "Tell me your 'experience,' Jon." His shadowed fingers made quotation marks.

The sarcastic tone in Dan's voice prompted Jean to glance at Spence, a warning for him not react. The silent exchange wasn't missed by Brick.

Jon moved to reach in his pocket and froze, listening to an amplified announcement of Kip Forrester's voice echoing through the trees:

"You're in for a surprise tonight, my friends. Nowhere else will you be able to hear the legendary Legs Flanders and Wheezy Beevers. Pass the champagne and give them both a big hand!"

Applause erupted, punctuated by the tinkle of crystal.

"They're all outside the back of the house," Jean whispered.

"I gotta go. This has to wait," Jon urged. "Jean and Spence, come with me. The boys are about to play. I missed Hughes when he arrived. Dammit, Brick!" He smacked the steering wheel and opened his door.

Jean churned her hand at Spence to get out of the car to catch up to Jon. "You two stay here," she instructed. "We need to help Jon."

Her heels clicked on the asphalt as she followed Spence. She flinched at the *phoomph* of two more doors on the Crown Vic.

Jon put a finger to his lips as he stepped into the entryway. Spence stuck behind Jon, but Jean held back to do a looky-loo. She had been itching to get inside the house to check out Kip's taste in decorating. Except for the clank of dishes in the kitchen, there was no sign of life in the downstairs.

The aroma of roasted fish and freshly baked bread floated through the rooms. Jean scanned the expansive living room to the right. A leather couch, upholstered in a warm chestnut tone, wrapped the space in a horseshoe. Large sprays of bright yellow sassafras branches, threaded with tiny white lights, reached out from ceramic floor vases placed around the room. The spread screamed money. Kip clearly had better taste in decorating a room than he had in putting together an outfit. She stood transfixed until she heard the din of chatter outside. Turning back to the front door, Jean waved her hands for Brick and Anhur Kumar to stay quiet.

She met up with Spence at the open back patio doors. Jean grasped Spence's arm and led him out to the patio, where they slipped into the gathering unnoticed. The final notes of Wheezy's masterful styling of Benny Goodman's version of "Moonglow" danced among the glittery dresses. Several guests started to whistle. Wheezy took a bow.

Mixed with the applause, familiar voices in a building argument caught Jean's attention. Dan, Jon, and Anhur had receded to a border of hydrangea bushes behind the guests. The white blossoms re-sembled cheerleader pom-poms.

"Don't push me on this, Brick!" Jon's voice failed to contain his anger.

"You're pushing *me*," Brick countered. "That video shows the Collinses with the fabric. That thing moved and changed!"

"You have no idea what you're dealing with."

With widened eyes, Jean tried to get their attention. Only Anhur met her gaze. She motioned for him to intervene and turned back to face the stage.

Kip lifted the microphone from its stand with the harmonica gripped in his other hand.

"Ladies and gentlemen, I'm about to reunite this priceless har-monica, first owned by Muddy Waters, with a legend. The instrument is one of my recent acquisitions, but I am a collector second to being a fan. I'm thrilled to say we have a surprise for you tonight. Please welcome my close, personal friend…Legs Flanders!"

With long steps into the glare from a spotlight mounted on the side of the house, Legs took the handheld microphone from Kip. As he shook Kip's hand, Jean released a breath as the harp slipped into his fingers. Legs waved it above his head. Trying to catch a glimpse, the guests raised their eyes in fascination. Jean cheered along with them. Legs gave the guests a broad smile and a salute, Jean knew, that was meant for her and Spence. Legs lowered himself onto a folding chair, hastily set up for his appearance. Behind him, Wheezy's expression was triumphant that they still had what it took to get a crowd excited.

"Are you ready?" Legs shouted.

"Ready!" the crowd called back.

"You ready for me?"

"Ready!"

Wheezy fluttered the top keys with some background phrases to keep the audience stoked.

"My friend, Willie Dixon, wrote a special song. This harp is the one Muddy use back in 1954 to record the number I'm gonna do. Been thinkin' about this one all day."

The instrument glinted in the light as he raised it to his mouth over the microphone. His hands shivered a long high note of introduction. Two-fingered whistles from the audience punctuated the evening air.

Legs started singing "I'm Ready," the lumbering beat a perfect match for his deep voice. Bodies began to sway. After a few minutes, the patio became a dance floor.

"They're still fighting back there," Jean said, leaning toward Spence. The absent nod he returned indicated he was lost in the music. "Jon's getting heated. Stay here."

"Okay…" Spence plucked a glass of champagne from a passing tray and took a sip.

Jean retreated behind the crowd to eavesdrop on Jon, Dan, and Anhur.

"Please, gentlemen, calm down," Anhur warned and held out his hands. "Emotions create energy." His eyes fixed on Jean's for help; everyone else's was fixed on Legs.

CHAPTER 19

Is There a Doctor in the House?

Jon stared at Brick. Something extraordinary had caused this unprofessional showdown of wills. Jon was stumped and Anhur had been rendered somewhat speechless by the display.

"What is with you, Dan? Get a damned grip," Jon seethed through gritted teeth.

"If you saw the same recording I did, you wouldn't—" Brick stopped when Jon held up his hand and pointed.

Forrester set his empty champagne flute on a passing tray. With his hands in his pockets, Kip sauntered toward them with a furrowed brow. He stopped in front of the three of them and studied their faces, the last being Jon's.

"Who are you? Were you invited here?"

"Your timing is perfect, Mr. Forrester. I need to speak with you," Jon said. He reached in his breast pocket and showed Kip his credentials. "Special Agent Jon Sergert, FBI. Is there a place we can talk?"

"This is my home, Mr. Segert. I'm having a party. You weren't *invited.*" Kip's stance signaled his readiness to defend his turf. He rubbed his chin and pointed. "Who are these other two?"

"Special Agent Dan Brick, FBI," Dan said, pulling out his ID.

Kip licked his lips, the only hint a chord had been struck.

"And you?" He pointed to Kumar.

"Anhur Kumar. I am the director of the Cairo Museum."

"What the hell? If you gentlemen have something to say to me, then make an appointment at my office."

"Let's talk inside." Jon nodded for Kip to follow him in the house and took three steps toward the French doors. Not hearing movement behind him, Jon turned back around.

Kip stood stock-still, appearing to be self-conscious. But his guests didn't care if he stripped naked; their attention was focused on the music. Well, almost all of his guests. Jon noticed a man who had to be Dr. Hughes standing at the far edge of the bouncing crowd, and his attention was locked on the four of them. Jon smirked at him.

Jon approached Kip with his hands spread. "Okay, then. We'll do this right here." He pointed his finger at Brick to his left. "Back me up."

"You've got three minutes." Kip crossed his arms, his lips tense. "When these guys finish their set, I'm done with you."

Jon leaned toward Kip, close enough to be nauseated by his heavy cologne. "Got any titty pills?"

Kip's eyes widened as the conversation in the restaurant raced across his face. He broke Jon's gaze to search the crowd.

"Looking for Winthrop? Dr. Sniffles?"

"Get out," Kip fumed, his face flushing to scarlet. "I want you—all of you—to leave. Now!" He swept his hand in a karate chop and straightened his jacket. He moved to walk away, but Jon grabbed his sleeve.

"Not without you and Hughes in tow. I have a warrant for your arrest. The police are out front waiting for both of you."

"For *what?*"

"Collusion, insider trading, plus a host of other charges. The whole conversation at a certain Palamino Restaurant was riveting. It justified a warrant for your and Hughes's arrest in two seconds flat."

Kip's jaw tightened as the flush in his face drained to chalk white.

"A wire?" he said, his voice escalating above the music.

"Giddyap." Jon turned. "Brick, will you go and tell the officers to join us?" Jon wrapped his fingers around the talon in his pocket in case Kip stepped up his anger.

Brick grabbed Jon's arm and addressed Kip.

"Give us a minute."

"Are you demented?" Jon said, incredulous. "I'm about to—"

"I'm not your errand boy." Brick snatched the leather pouch from Anhur's right hand. "But I want to know what you did to Coulter with *this*!"

Jon's stared in disbelief as Brick pulled back the flap and yanked out the fabric. He scrunched the cloth and shook it. Jon whipped out the talon and pointed the curved tip at him, as if a gun.

Shock and horror washed over Anhur's face. "Stop! You must not—"

Kip retreated and froze, his eyes shifting from the fabric to the talon.

Jean lunged seemingly from out of nowhere. She wedged herself between Dan and Jon with one hand on each of their chests.

"Whoa. Whoa. Whoa! This isn't the time or place to have a fight about this!" she ordered. "Jon, calm down. Brick, give the fabric back to Anhur! Spence, keep the guys playing!"

The altercation had indeed drawn attention. The music slowed as Legs and Wheezy threw a concerned gaze at the commotion. Spence whirled his hand for them to continue. Wheezy stepped up the tempo, and Legs closed his eyes to start the harmonica solo, the intensity of which startled the crowd. Heads turned forward.

Jon sensed a curious vibration in his chest. He stared down at Jean's hand, her wedding ring flashing in the light. She vibrated too. He followed the length of her arm to her other hand on Brick's chest. The vibration shook all three of them. With the talon in his hand, he tried to move her hand with his fingers, but it wouldn't budge.

A thin blue line of electricity shot between the talon and the fabric. Tiny orbs undulated along the connection. Jean stared, in shock, as they passed in front of her chest.

At the peak of Legs's solo, electric-blue light erupted from the harmonica. A triangle of blue, pulsing lasers shot from the light, connecting the harmonica, the fabric in Brick's hand, and the talon in Jon's fingers. Heads ducked and followed the laser beams. Jean stared in shock and started to shake.

"What the hell is happening?" Jean shouted. Her hands were covered with veins of blue light. Spence bolted to her side, but took a step back as his gaze trailed from one of her sparking hands to the other.

Electricity coursed through Jon's chest. He couldn't pull the talon away as long as the blue lightning connected it to the harmonica and the fabric—through Jean. He broke his gaze from her and locked it on Brick. He'd never seen Brick's eyes open so wide.

"Wh...wh...what are you...do—" Brick stuttered, unable to continue.

"Nothing! Not me! Jean, pull...your...hands away."

"I...can't!"

Anhur moved to stand in front of Jean and signaled Spence to stand back. He cupped her face with his hands. In a calm voice, he said: "*Think*, Jean. Why did you and Spence do what you did for Mary Coulter? *Speak to me.*" His intense gaze fixed on hers.

"She...wanted...to be...with her family." Tears welled in Jean's eyes, spilling on Anhur's fingers.

"Why? Tell me."

"Lost...her husband...devastated."

"She loved him. Yes?"

"Yes..."

"You and Spencer filled her with the ability to love again."

Jon gawked as the color of the electricity changed from blue to neon green, undulating and sparking. The veins of lightning straightened to solid lines. Jean squeezed her eyes and tipped her head back, unable to contain the emotion.

"Look at me, Jean. Who do *you* love more than anyone else?"

"Sp...Spence."

"And how long will this love last?"

"For...ever...eternity."

Anhur closed his eyes. "Eternity," he whispered, nodding his agreement.

Jon turned his gaze to the crowd, having no idea what was happening. But he knew it was important. Disgust filled him as the guests continued to smile and laugh at the light show. They applauded, thinking the effect was part of an arranged act. The guests stepped back to form a loose circle around the three of them.

A deep, ethereal hum, as that from a blown transformer, raised the hair on his arms. The air felt magnetized. Jon struggled to inhale as the energy raced to his fingers.

The talon exploded into a cloud of dissipating steam.

The shock wave knocked Jean to the concrete, breaking the connection. Sparking fire shot into the air from the fabric and swirled in loops above their heads. Flames gathered to form the shape of a hawk, nearly six feet across. Jon's gaze followed the blazing image. The fiery, outstretched wings boiled with blue and gold light as the image soared above the crowd, swooping over Wheezy and Legs. The hawk circled the patio as the audience applauded.

"Horus!" Jon shouted.

"Jean!" Spence grabbed her arm too late to break her fall.

"I'm...okay." Jean squeezed her eyes as Spence lifted her to her feet.

"Wooo! Wooo!" The guests ducked and cheered as the shaped fire passed.

"My hands! Something is...happening!" Brick stared, horrified, at the fabric.

The phoenixes stirred and strained against the cloth. Their wings broke from the surface, stretching as if emerging out of a shell. Dan stepped backward as the birds stilled and faded. They disappeared; his fingers went limp. The empty fabric fell to the patio. Brick shook as he opened and closed his hands. Anhur lunged for the cloth. He searched the flowers and vines and found only three empty spaces left behind.

A flash of color made Jon turn toward the lawn beyond the patio. Shocks of gold, turquoise, red, and orange feathers glinted in the reflected lights twenty feet away. Wings *whooshed* as the phoenixes launched in sequence. Jon's gaze followed their flight until they became one with the night sky. He turned and met Brick's wild stare.

"They've flown. Gone!" Jon struggled to take a breath.

Anhur stared the empty fabric.

The music stopped. Heads whipped to the front in the sudden silence. Jon's gaze followed to the source of everyone's attention.

Legs collapsed from the folding chair, toppling like Pick-up Sticks. The harmonica clattered to the concrete and slid to a stop under the piano bench. On his knees, Wheezy pulled himself toward Legs.

"Noooo!" Jean shouted and pushed through the crowd. "A doctor! We need a doctor!"

Jean turned with pleading eyes to Dr. Braxton Hughes as he threw off his black dinner jacket and rolled up his sleeves. He stood next to Legs and motioned for her to move out of the way.

"I'm a doctor," he said. "Let me see what I can do."

"Save him!" Jean held out her hands to Spence as he pushed to the front of the crowd and knelt next to her. She clenched his sleeve. "Call an ambulance. I don't have my phone."

"Already did. I had mine. I think one of the officers called too."

Jon knelt next to her and studied Braxton Hughes. "They did. The ambulance is on the way. He tilted his head toward Hughes. "Jean, that's him. He's the one in the deal with Kip."

Hughes glared at Jon. "You want me to work on him or not?"

"Yes! Hurry!" Jean shouted.

Hughes rolled Legs on his back and compressed his chest in rhythmic pumps. "Stay calm. This is about patience and perseverance more than skill." He gave Kip a nervous glance as he approached and stood next to him.

"Do you know what you're doing?" she asked, brushing away the tears on her cheek. Jean wasn't sure if the top of Hughes's head glistened from the warm night air or the lack of confidence. She suspected the latter.

"Of course he does," Kip chided, monitoring the situation with his hands on his hips. He seemed more concerned about his party being ruined than he was for Legs's condition. He turned and studied her. "And who are you here with?"

Jean glared at him. "I ought to punch you in the face! This is your fault!"

Wheezy turned and crawled to the piano bench to retrieve the harmonica. Kip stepped beside him, knelt on one knee, and extended his hand. "I'll take that," he said, pointing to the instrument.

"The hell you will! You'd have to cut off my hands first." Wheezy pulled back a knuckled fist and coldcocked Kip in the face. Blood splattered down the front of his cream-colored jacket.

"Ahhhhh!" Kip fell backward and bumped into Jon, who lifted him to his feet.

"Nice one, Wheezy." Jon tightened his grip on Kip's arm. "Let's go, Forrester."

"Sit back. Give him room!" Hughes continued to press and release, sweat dripping from his face. He raised his eyes to watch Kip being led away.

"Where's the damned ambulance? He's not a real doctor!" Jean challenged, squeezing Legs's hand. "Can you hear me, Legs?"

Hughes stood, wiped his chin, and reached for his jacket. "He does need a hospital. I can't do much here."

"The paramedics are on the way," Spence said, rubbing her arms. "This is no one's fault."

"Oh yes, it is!" Jean threw off Spence's hand and stood. Filling her lungs with air, her tear-filled eyes blazed at Hughes. She stalked him, shaking with fury.

Hughes backed away, raising his hands to protect his face.

"What! Too much liability?" Jean pushed his chest with both

hands. "You're more concerned about yourself than saving this man. You greedy coward!"

The doctor froze. He stared at her, bracing for his own bloody nose. "I...I can't do any more."

"You don't *want* to do any more!" She punched his shoulder with her fist. "You fraud!"

Hughes stared at her, saying nothing in his defense. Spence had his arm around her waist, holding her back.

Jon emerged from the house with two officers in tow. One grasped the doctor's arms, the other cuffed his wrists.

"I hope you rot in jail!" Jean shouted as Hughes was escorted out.

Sirens blared in the distance, growing louder as the ambulance raced up the driveway. A strobe of red lights reflected down the hall from the open front door.

Four paramedics wearing blue latex gloves streamed to the patio with a defibrillator. An intricate curative ballet commenced as they worked on Legs.

Anhur stepped behind her. "The phoenixes have flown, Jean."

Through a veil of tears, she turned and met his gaze. "I know," she whispered. "Who released them?"

She followed the path of Anhur's finger as he pointed to the dark hedge of hydrangea bushes. In the shadows stood Dan Brick, staring at his hands.

"Go with Legs. I'll meet you at the hospital!" Jon shouted.

Jean, Spence, and Wheezy followed the stretcher out the front door toward the ambulance. As they moved, Legs moaned, and his eyes fluttered. Jean's heart fluttered in response, but this weak revival also served to refocus her to the reality of the situation.

"Brick! He needs to come with us!" Jean turned and bolted back through the house. She spotted Anhur talking to Dan. Anhur's hands gripped Dan's shoulders. "You have to come with Legs, Dan. He's in your hands! Anhur, take Brick's car and follow us to the hospital."

Dan raised his eyes to her in disbelief.

"He's what?"

"Hurry!" Jean pulled Brick's arm. "Give Anhur your keys!"

As if in a trance, Dan reached in his jacket pocket. The keys jingled as they fell to the patio; he couldn't hold on to the fob. Anhur picked them up. Jean rushed him through the house and toward the ambulance. Most of the guests had left the party, with only a handful standing outside with morbid curiosity.

"Get in, Jean. I'll drive Anhur!" Spence called out and bolted to Brick's car.

Wheezy had already planted himself next to Legs in the ambulance, attempting to keep him engaged. In the farthest corner, Brick sat on the bench. He splayed his fingers across his knees. The doors slammed behind Jean.

"Stay out of the way," the paramedic said, attaching a heart monitor to Legs's chest. "I think there are too many of you in here."

"You don't understand. We have to be in here, especially him." Jean pointed to Brick, who raised his eyes in bewilderment. She turned back to Legs. "He'll be okay, right?"

The paramedic offered her only a slight shake of his head, an answer Jean couldn't read.

"Hey, old man. You were the life of the party." Wheezy patted Legs's arm.

"On...my way, Wheez," Legs whispered, his voice barely audible.

"Yeah, we're going to the hospital to get you fixed up. Gonna be just fine."

Legs reached up and pulled the mask under his chin, despite the protest from the paramedic.

"If this...the big one, then...Rosey's waitin for me, yes, she is."

"Stop talking nonsense. The only big one is the kick I'm going to give your bony butt. Don't mess with me, Legs. I punched a guy for you tonight. Felt good too." Wheezy inspected his red knuckles and showed them to the technician. "Do you have an ice pack?"

Jean reached up and slipped Legs's mask back on his face. Her gaze fixed on the monitor, following each beat, hoping the next one wouldn't be his last.

The ambulance sped down the hill toward the city center. The driver switched on the siren. Dan leaned his head against the side panel and closed his eyes.

CHAPTER 20

It's All About the Music

The ambulance pulled under the bay at Emergency. The back doors burst open and the paramedics whisked Legs out. Jean emerged and helped Wheezy down the steep incline, followed by Brick. A hush parted the automatic glass panels. The three of them watched Legs disappear.

"Let's wait out here for Spence and Anhur." As Jean said the words, she spotted Brick's Crown Victoria pulling into the parking lot. Wheezy reached up and patted her back for reassurance.

"Legs wouldn't want you making a fuss over him. He's ready for anything," he said.

Jean turned and wiped her eyes. "What?"

"Why do you think he chose to play that song at the party? He told me before we left DC. This trip was a kind of last hoorah for him. He's had heart problems for three years now."

"He didn't say a word."

"Just the way Legs is. He may be famous, but he hates the attention unless he's playing."

"Are there any family members we need to notify?"

"I'm his executor. No family left. He had a brother, but he died back in eight-two. I'm it, Jean. Let's go in. I want to see Legs."

"What about you? No holding out on us, Wheezy."

"Nah. I'm healthy as a horse. I'm old. I'm rich. I'm short. And I got my best friend right in here." He made a little fist and thumped his chest.

Jean marveled at Wheezy's calm handling of the dire situation that was unfolding, but it wasn't an unfamiliar sight. She had witnessed the behavior with her own elderly family members, as well as Spence's. Beyond the age of eighty, mysterious endorphins kicked in to shift the definition of grief to philosophical acceptance of life's circle. But she was in no way ready to let go of Legs…or Wheezy.

Brick stood at the edge of the group, shifting uncomfortably. An outcast. Anhur spread his hands to gather everyone together.

"Come inside. Let us all find a quiet place to talk," he said. "Given the circumstances, we have much to discuss. Yes?"

Jean turned to Brick. "Are you okay, Dan?"

"I don't know. What's going on in my goddamned hands?"

At the counter of an adjacent waiting area, Anhur spoke in a quiet voice to a staff volunteer. The woman appeared to be in her sixties. The expression on her sweet face indicated she'd been hypnotized by Anhur's exotic charm. Jean figured he could ask her to walk across hot coals and she would have gladly obliged. Smoothing the front of her pink smock, she stepped from behind the counter to address the group.

"Mr. Kumar has informed me of your situation. I'm so sorry. He tells me that you need some privacy. I perfectly understand. My name is Grace."

Jean followed Grace as she ushered them into a small conference room used mostly for difficult and private discussions with families, she guessed. Grace switched on the light.

"You can use this as long as you'd like," she said. "I'll tell the doctor where you'll be when he comes out to give you an update."

"I want to go back and sit with him," Wheezy declared. From his tone, negotiation wasn't an option. Jean had a vision of him punching Grace in the nose if she responded with any guff.

Grace pursed her lips in response. "Follow me, but only one person is allowed in intensive care at a time."

As Wheezy followed the woman, he turned and waved the harmonica at the group.

Jean, Spence, Anhur, and Brick pulled out chairs. Anhur set the fabric in the center of the table and spread the folds. They stared at the vines and tiny flowers on the cream-colored background, studying the significance of the blank spaces.

"I'm glad Wheezy's not here for this conversation," Spence said.

"Still empty." Jean tried to keep her voice quiet. She glanced at Dan.

"Mrs. Collins, you did something to this. What happened?" Brick said, regaining an official tone.

"Did you feel electricity in your hands when Legs collapsed?" Jean ran her finger around the edge of the fabric. "You released the power of this. You don't understand what amazing capabilities you now have. You can make Legs immortal if, or when, the time comes. Let's hope you don't need to use it." She uttered the words but couldn't cover the inevitability of the choice.

Brick turned to Anhur. "Is she right about this?"

"Yes. The Collinses experienced the transformation themselves. She speaks from experience. You witnessed the same process on the recording."

"You showed him the video you made of us in Cairo?" Shock streaked across Spence's face.

"I'm afraid it became necessary in order to impress upon our skeptical friend here the seriousness of the situation."

"Who did you make immortal?" Brick asked, clearly verifying information he already knew. His expression remained hard. She'd hoped, by now, his shell had softened.

"Raleigh Coulter's mother…Mary."

"How? What did you do?"

"Once the phoenixes have flown, the ability is inside you until you release their power for the dying person. We released them so

Spence and I had the ability to make her immortal. Anhur showed us the instructions, written in hieroglyphs in Nefertari's tomb. You set your hands on the person before it happens. Timing is crucial. That's why Spence and I had to rush back from Cairo. We needed to get home before Mary died. We arrived just in time."

"Where is she, then? Call her here."

"She's not a dog, Brick," Spence snapped.

"She may be in this room now." Jean motioned for Spence to stay calm. "Mary can choose to reveal herself or not. But be prepared, Dan. The magic lingers even after you've released it."

"What exactly killed Raleigh? I know you have the answer, Jean." Dan flexed his fingers, seemingly wanting but not wanting the explanation.

"Horus," she whispered. "The talon in Jon's hand at the party came from the manifestation of his form as a hawk."

Anhur leaned back in his chair. "The fabric transformed to protect Agent Segert and the Collinses," he explained. "You witnessed the Egyptian god, in yet a different form, this evening."

"How did Segert get that talon?"

"After Horus attacked Raleigh, he disappeared, but his claw remained behind, stuck in Raleigh's thigh." Jean shrugged. "A fluke of magical nature."

"So a hawk did kill Raleigh Coulter?"

"If you want to put that in the report to close the investigation, go right ahead," Spence warned, tapping the table, "but you should think long and hard about explaining what you witnessed at the party or on the recording from Cairo."

In response, Brick leaned away from the fabric, as if distance would maintain objectivity. The posture didn't work. His hands were shaking.

"And the lights? How did those happen?"

"I don't know. Altogether new." Jean turned to Anhur. "Can you explain that phenomenon? The lights happened at the festival too, when Legs played the harmonica."

Silence settled over the table as Anhur's deep gaze fixed on each of them in sequence. "As you say, this is new. Possibly the skill Mr. Flanders exhibited when he played the instrument opened a higher dimension and connected to the power in the fabric and the talon. His talent created powerful emotion, which in turn released extreme energy. You, Jean, acted as a conduit—a highway—for it to travel. Only a theory."

"Figure out how to write *that* in a report, Dan," Spence added.

Brick shook his head. "Put the cloth away."

"We will need to find a safe place to keep this," Anhur said. "Do you have any suggestions? It cannot come back to Cairo with me."

"The Portland Museum of Art," Spence offered. "I'll call the curator when we get home."

Anhur nodded in agreement, his wheels turning. "Of course. A temporary loan. Other precious objects also need protection. I am more than willing to meet with their board to discuss the possibility of an expanded exhibit."

"I bet we can make that happen."

Jean flinched and glanced at her watch. It was after eleven o'clock. "Spence, we need to call Dillon to go over to the house and feed Mycroft. We could be here for days, unless we arrange for Legs to be transferred to Milwaukie Hospital."

Anhur folded the fabric as Spence stepped out of the room.

"Now you know everything, Dan. Only you have the power to make Legs immortal if the time comes. You released the phoenixes. You're the one who can do it." Jean paused and blew out a breath. "On second thought, you don't know everything. You need to meet an immortal, I guess. There's a whole clan, including a hundred-year-old dog, which happens to be quite fond of our cat."

Brick's mouth opened.

A tap on the door ceased further conversation. A young doctor entered, his expression void of clues to Legs's prognosis. From his youthful, unlined skin and clear pale eyes, he must be a first-year intern, Jean thought. The embroidered words on the pocket of his white coat said: *Dr. Robert Brooks, Cardiologist.*

"Are any of you family?" he asked.

Spence stepped back in the room and gave Jean a nod. He sat and took her hand. "He'll be at the house in about half an hour," he whispered.

"My husband and I are like family," Jean said to the doctor, squeezing Spence's fingers to brace for the news.

"Mr. Flanders sustained significant damage to his heart. The valve is not functioning, and blood isn't pumping efficiently." Dr. Brooks made a circle of his thumb and forefinger, flexing it. "In other words, his ticker's plain worn out."

"Can you replace the valve? They do those procedures all the time these days."

"Too much damage. The combination of his age and the trauma to his heart doesn't make him a candidate for surgery. His body wouldn't be able to handle anything invasive." He blew out a breath. "More skilled care was needed at the time of the heart event, before the paramedics arrived. Even speed might not have made any difference. The damage is irreversible. The goal at this juncture is to keep him as comfortable as possible for the next twenty-four hours. We need to take one step at a time."

Jean admired the doctor's ability to be direct without coming off as a cold fish. At least Dr. Brooks wasn't offering a course of false hope punctuated with dollar signs. Her father suffered miserably with congestive heart failure. Only days before he died, another doctor had scheduled him to undergo surgery for cataracts.

"How long does he have?" Spence asked.

"Hard to say. The will to live isn't a science. Something we'll never be able to completely understand. You should be prepared, though, for every possibility."

Possibilities. Jean now imagined herself taking over the case, prepared to offer much more than Dr. Brooks could have imagined. "Is he awake? Can we see him?"

"He is. Just you and your husband for right now, though. His friend is with him and keeping his spirits up." The doctor chuckled and rubbed his brow. "He's terrorizing the nurses. I'm sure they'll welcome you with open arms."

"I will wait here," Anhur said.

"We want this man to come with us too." Jean slid her hand across the table and patted the wood in front of Brick.

Jean pumped two squirts from the bottle of hand sanitizer mounted on the wall outside of Legs's room. Her nod to Spence and Dan indicated they should do the same. Flexing the muscles in her face, she attempted to mask her concern with a broad smile as she stepped inside. Legs didn't need stress and boo-hoos.

"Hey, guys! Keep the noise down to dull roar," she announced to Legs and Wheezy. "You'll upset the other patients." She set her purse on the built-in desk.

"Come on in. We're continuing the party in here," Wheezy said. He sat at the bottom of Legs's bed with his wingtips dangling over the side as he perused a menu. The harmonica in his lap appeared to be another visitor in the room.

Legs rested with an oxygen mask on his face. His eyelids opened like a curtain for him to take a bow. The weak waves on the monitor above his head immediately drew Jean's gaze. Among all the other pulsing signals and numbers, that one was hard to miss.

"You can order anything whenever you want. No set feeding times. All this heart-healthy stuff is boring, though." Wheezy reached for the phone. "Hi, this is room three-oh-three. Mr. Flanders would like the chicken nuggety things; cottage cheese and tomato—the chunky kind, not the creamy; and the fruit cup for dessert—fresh, not canned. Hurry, he's hungry." He hung up and laughed. "What are *faux poussin* tenders?"

"Probably tofu. Tastes just like underdone chicken," Spence quipped, mirroring the attempt to keep the mood upbeat.

Jean's gaze settled on Legs. She grasped his hand. "How are you doing?"

"I'm doin', not livin'." His voice sounded muffled from behind the mask.

"You've got some challenges, no doubt."

Legs pulled the oxygen mask from his face. It blew life at his Adam's apple. "Challenges." He attempted to chuckle but coughed. "I got one sittin' on my bed."

"He's making sure the nurses stay in line."

When Wheezy examined the breakfast side of the menu, Jean leaned toward Legs to whisper in his ear. "Do you want to live forever?"

"Aw, Crazy Eyes, I think I know…what you mean. I done more livin' in the last week than I deserve. Thank you for that."

"No pain. No stuck valves. No medicine. Make music forever. You have a choice."

"Honey…not our call," Spence warned, stepping behind her. "Legs, this is an important decision, but it's yours to make alone."

"Forever is forever."

None of the conversation was missed by Wheezy. He remained quiet, pretending to focus on the menu.

Jean glanced at Brick, who sat in the leather reclining chair in front of the window. The air rippled next to him. Brick studied the undulating images, incredulous. Two human forms gathered strength and clarity until Doc and Jess stood next to him. Brick recoiled at the sight. From behind his wire-rimmed glasses, Doc assessed Brick, rubbing his chin. Brick sucked in a breath and flinched when Doc patted his shoulder. The first time to meet an immortal was, no doubt, a jolt.

"I hoped you'd come!" Jean rushed to both immortal men. Their hazy outlines encompassed Jean as she embraced each of them. The same effect resulted as Spence shook their hands.

"So this is the famous Lawrence Flanders," Doc said and stepped to the side of the bed. Jess followed.

"Hey, he's the man in the painting," Wheezy declared. "He likes your cat."

"'*Loves* their cat' is a more accurate description, Mr. Beevers." Doc gave Wheezy a sly smile that melted to tenderness as he studied Legs. "Mr. Flanders, I am privileged to make your acquaintance."

"Finest blower they is layin' in front of you, Doc," Jess said. "Caught you, Legs, in '58. Can I hold the harp?"

Legs struggled to lift his finger, capped with a pulse monitor. He pointed to Wheezy, who hadn't let the harmonica out of his sight since Legs had been admitted, not even to order food.

"Gotta wrestle it away from Wheez. We had a time tonight, yes, we did," Legs muttered.

Reluctant, Wheezy handed the harmonica to Jess but didn't take his eyes off the immortals. Doc never shifted his gaze from Legs.

The hazy outline of Doc's hand trailed as he rested it over Legs's. The heart monitor showed erratic lines as they made contact. A mechanical alarm blared.

"Spence, kindly stop the noise coming out of the box," Doc instructed. His voice remained calm. "No need for the intrusion."

Jean stepped away to give Spence room to fiddle with the machine. "I'll only turn the volume down. The nurses monitor the equipment. They'll come tearing in here."

"Do what you will." Doc's deep-brown eyes relaxed as the alarm quieted. "Machines can't tell anything of a man's wishes and desires. And wires certainly can't connect to a soul."

Jean nodded for Brick to come closer to Legs. She sensed the atmosphere in the room change as Doc studied Legs's tired, lined face. The cardiologist was right. He was worn out.

"You are fortunate to have a choice," Doc continued. "Only a select few get an option."

"All about a woman, Doc...and my kids," Legs whispered. "Rosey is waitin' for me. Wheezy be fine."

"A might ironic. I made the same choice because of my Charlotte. She waited for me too, but in immortality. We are more aligned than you realize, Mr. Flanders."

"Too lonely…knowin' she on one side…me on the other." Legs let out a heavy sigh. "Can't."

"Are you sure, Legs? The birds have flown." Jean stepped to the other side of the bed. She inspected the growth ridges on Legs's fingernails, like the rings marking his time as a musical genius. His hand squeezed hers.

"You two are somethin'. I feel it in your hands. Doing good things with 'em."

Legs was slipping from her grasp. Jean felt helpless against the insurmountable power of choice. Her gaze searched for Spence. When it found him, his eyes burned with the same resignation.

No one else in the room could comprehend Doc's over 150 years of knowledge. His words came back to her when she and Spence visited Richmond: *touch can be more powerful than pills.* Jean set aside her own wishes, embarrassed by her selfishness. She would have made the same choice if Spence wasn't with her. This process wasn't about what she wanted; the priority was what Legs wanted. Her throat burned with the truth.

As if listening to her thoughts, Doc nodded. He turned and stepped toward Dan, whose eyes widened.

"Give me your hands, son."

Dan's fingers shook as he reached out to Doc and studied the man: tousled gray hair, deeply lined face, vested suit cut from the cloth of a different time. Brick's expression reflected his struggle between rational thought and empirical evidence of the fantastic.

"So this is all true?"

"It is."

"And Jon Segert has known about you?"

"Certainly. I did enjoy working with him to catch that Dromov scoundrel. Jess helped him get back the harmonica too."

"Why wouldn't he tell me?"

"Can you, yourself, find the words? Best ponder on what you know, Mr. Brick."

Dan seemed fascinated by the illumination of his hands when

they touched Doc's. Jean studied Dan's expression as it changed into nearly a smile, or maybe enlightenment that life wasn't what he thought it was. Today, a transformation did take place, just not the one she anticipated.

"You hold on to the gift you've been given until you're ready to give it away. Changes your view, it will, but not here...not now." Doc gazed at Wheezy but didn't release Dan's hands. "Mr. Beevers, you take good care. I'm sure we shall see each other again soon."

"What did you show him?" Wheezy asked, straightening his thick glasses.

"Life, Wheez," Legs whispered. "Things you only know...when you is right where I'm layin'."

Doc faded and disappeared; the mist of his visage swirled over Dan's suspended hands like dissipating smoke.

Jess handed the harmonica back to Wheezy. Tiny sparks blew out of the mouthpiece before it left his grip. "I think you be livin' forever, anyway," Jess said and winked. "Every time somebody put one-a your records on, you be coming alive again."

"I thank you for that," Legs whispered and squeezed Jean's hand. In turn, she reached her other one out to Spence.

"Are you really sure?" A moment of panic closed her throat. A blanket of reality warmed her core as it wrapped around her.

"Gotta know, darlin'...they throw you outta...the band...when you can't...keep a...beat..."

Legs closed his eyes. His fingers went limp in hers. Jess faded, and with him the silent peaks on the monitor smoothed to a straight line.

Letting go. Jean turned to meet the pain of it in Spence's face. No tears—only appreciation for the brief bright light Legs had brought into their lives, forever enriching them because he had passed through. She stroked Wheezy's shoulder as he held Legs's harmonica, turning it over and over in his fingers.

Brick rested his head in his hands. "What the hell do I do now?"

A deep breath seemed impossible as she struggled to offer a

response. *Tasks. A list. Rational thought.* "Dan, can you go find Anhur? Spence and I will help Wheezy handle the arrangements here and meet you downstairs."

Dan stood and held Legs's feet beneath the cotton blanket as though he could bring him back to life. The flow of energy was blocked. "I'd better call Jon."

Wheezy put the harmonica to his lips and handed it to Spence; he did the same and held it out to Jean. She warmed the instrument with her lips too, leaned over Legs, and kissed his forehead.

Two nurses burst through the door.

CHAPTER 21

Flying Solo

Jon stared at Braxton Hughes and Kip Forrester from across the table in the interviewing room at the police station. Muffled moaning wafted down the hall from some addict writhing on a cot, his face probably buried in a blanket. Jon nodded his head for the Seattle police officer to push the door closed.

Legs was lying in a hospital bed fighting for his life. These two men in front of him were no more than petty thieves in fancy clothes, stealing lives without a second thought. Resentment filled Jon from the inside out. They didn't care about Legs, Wheezy, or anyone else besides themselves. From the haughty expressions on their faces, Jon figured Kip and Braxton believed they would breeze out of this. All a mistake. A misunderstanding. One call to their lawyers and they'd be finishing their deal.

Out of habit, Jon stuck his hand in his jacket pocket. The talon was gone forever. He had to do this alone, with hollow insides. He pulled out a pen and rolled it between his fingers. Rancor strengthened to resolve as he interpreted the smug expressions on the two men's faces.

"How long is this going to take?" Kip sneered, dabbing his nose. He checked the rust-spotted tissue for fresh bleeding. "You ruined an important party—an expensive party, I might add. I'll sue you if any clients walk because of this charade."

"Only one charade is going on here—the one you and Hughes are trying to pull."

"Do you know who I am?" Hughes huffed, inspecting his fingernails. He removed his black-framed glasses and gave them a sarcastic twirl.

"Oh, if I only had a nickel for every time a suspect asked that question."

"You're going to regret bringing me in here. The board members at Enzer are pretty powerful."

"Yes, they are. We had an interesting conversation. Or I should say, *you* did, by way of a certain recording from your luncheon last week. They thought it—what's the word—*enlightening*?" Jon waited for a reaction.

Hughes glared at Kip, who balled the bloody tissue in his fist.

"A business conversation, nothing more," Kip said to Jon while patting the air in front of Hughes to indicate that nothing was wrong. "You're not in the financial industry, so you don't understand how it works." He shifted his gaze to a black pen mark on the surface of the table. He licked his thumb and rubbed the slash to make the ink disappear. It only faded, slightly. He licked his thumb again and attacked the mark with a vigorous rub.

"You shouldn't do that. You might catch cold," Jon warned.

Hughes's expression erupted to fury. Jon expected him to haul off and finish the job Wheezy had started. "Did you record our conversation? Are you trying to blackmail me or something?"

"No, no. He's bluffing, Brax." Kip turned to Jon, pleading for reprieve. "Tell him you're bluffing, dammit! You're screwing up a perfectly legitimate business deal, Segert."

"Legitimate for whom? The average investor who thinks, *Hey, I've reviewed the financial statements. Enzer Pharmaceuticals is a company I should invest in for the long haul.*" Jon twisted his face. "Nash Winthrop didn't describe the process quite that way."

"Winthrop?" Hughes's bow tie tightened as his face flushed. "You ass! Did you and that weasel set me up?" A glisten of sweat coated his bald head.

Jon remained quiet. Forrester and Hughes at each other's throats produced a pretty good show. Reducing this interview to fisticuffs might speed things along.

"Not me! Must have been Winthrop." Kip's eyes settled on Jon. "Did you put a wire on him?"

Kip already knew, but had to make a show. Jon spread his hands, waiting for each of them to come up with the answer.

Loud enough for Hughes to hear, Kip muttered, "Nash didn't show up at the party."

"Why did I ever trust you, Forrester?" Hughes huffed. "You're not going to make a dime on this deal. I'll see to it." Hughes stood and straightened his dinner jacket.

"Sit down!" Jon demanded. "I tell *you* when this meeting is over."

Hughes sat and checked his cuff links. He refused to make eye contact.

"You're not making any money on your scam either. Insider trading is a serious charge; Enzer Pharmaceuticals thinks so too. In fact, they're anxious to meet with you to sign separation papers if you're convicted. They'll nullify the stock options, even the vested ones. Want me to schedule an appointment? Your calendar is wide open."

Shock streaked across Hughes's face. The emotion was genuine. The guy believed he'd done nothing wrong.

"I'll...sue your ass, Segert!" he shouted.

"For what? Causing a guilty conscience? Catching you selling information?"

"Defamation of character. This is my career...my reputation. You have no right."

"Shut up, Hughes." The smugness in Braxton's voice had worn out his last nerve. "Demanding payment from a third party in exchange for information under a confidentiality agreement is illegal. I know you don't respect the lines of ethics here, but the FBI does, and so do investors outside of your insider club."

Hughes crossed his arms, trying to act superior, but his tight face belied the weakness beneath the man's skin. Getting caught was definitely not in his plans.

Kip leaned forward, pressing on his sinuses to check for swelling. When he finally spoke, he sounded as though his nose had been plugged.

"What was going on with you, the other agent, and the Egyptian fellow? Some weird stuff. Freaky." Kip attempted to scramble the cards by changing the subject.

"I ask the questions, Forrester." Jon did a Shirley Temple tap dance inside but kept his demeanor all business.

"I want my harmonica back. That's my property. I paid a pretty penny too. Beevers stole it." Kip shook his finger. "And I'm pressing charges for assault. I'll probably need surgery."

Jon had to stop himself from reaching out and twisting the tip of Kip's nose. Instead, he narrowed his eyes and pined for Horus to show up and take a lethal bite.

"Stolen property," he said. "You deserved the punch. Couldn't have planted it better myself."

Kip grimaced. "I need to see a doctor."

Jon pointed to Hughes as his cell phone buzzed. "Check his nose." He glanced at the number. Brick. "Excuse me, gentlemen. Fight among yourselves for a moment." Jon kept his gaze on Hughes as he answered. Kip scratched at the dried blood on his jacket. "Hey, what's the update? What?" He pressed his forehead as his stomach dropped. "Is everyone okay? Drive them back to Portland. I'm wrapping up a few details. I'll be there as soon as I can. Brick, are you all right? You sound...yeah, we'll talk tomorrow."

Jon ended the call and ran his finger along the edge of his phone. He should have been at the hospital. He shut his eyes; the images of the missed developments scrolled past the inside of his lids. *Brick didn't follow through. Jean and Spence must be inconsolable. And Wheezy...poor Wheezy.* When Jon opened them, Kip and Braxton were staring at him with quizzical expressions, no doubt thinking the call was about them. In a way, it was.

"Are you a real doctor, Hughes?" Jon tried to stay composed.

"Of course! A ridiculous question!"

"I should add malpractice to the list of charges. Legs Flanders is dead because of you." He turned to the officer. "I'm done with this nonsense. Book 'em."

CHAPTER 22

Anhur's Wise Words

"Are you okay to drive, Dan?" Jean asked as the group entered the on ramp to I-5 south. "You've been awfully quiet since we left the hospital."

"This is a lot to absorb, Jean," Dan said, keeping his eyes forward.

Jean checked the digital clock on the dash: 4:00 a.m. The paperwork for death was much more intense than for birth, at least in emotion. Exhausting. At least Legs's body would follow them home in the next day or two. They'd arranged for a transfer to a funeral home they'd used for her father. Wheezy saw no reason to make arrangements in DC; Legs had wanted to be cremated. With friends and family gone, Wheezy's words that he was *it* made her want to keep him close.

Leaving the hospital had been gut-wrenching. Thank God for Anhur's cool head to keep them all on track. Brick had kept a stoic check on his emotions, but Jean knew he churned with conflict about the experience.

"Take a snooze, you guys," Brick said. "Me? I won't sleep for the next week."

"Wheezy, how are you doing?" Jean patted his knee. He held Legs's harmonica as if his old friend would fly out of the mouthpiece.

"I'm okay. I'm hungry." He glanced at her with a pained smile.

"I don't think I can sleep either, Dan. Maybe we should stop along the way." Jean swallowed hard. "We had this same conversation with Legs only this morning."

"His music survives," Spence said without turning around. "I'm going to do something special in the store as a tribute."

Anhur had been quiet, staring out the window. They all joined him in just looking. The waning moon cast unearthly shadows, which made the evergreens appear ominous. Puffs of clouds nested in the top branches.

"The trees are quite something here. Tall as Mr. Flanders," Anhur finally said. "They reach to the sky. I imagine some of them are hundreds of years old." Anhur turned to Jean. "Doctor Gaines sounds quite special. I would have very much enjoyed meeting him."

"He is. Was. The wisest man I've ever known, besides Spence, of course," Jean said, poking Spence's arm. "At some point, I'm sure you will. The next time we see him, we'll ask him to appear to you. He likes people who think at a higher level."

"I did have the privilege of meeting his daughter. Mary Coulter is a lovely woman."

"You did? When?"

"In my office in Cairo. She appeared to me."

"I want to meet her," Wheezy interjected.

"You will. Don't worry," Jean said. "I'm sure she'd love to meet you too."

"If not for Mary, I would not be here now," Anhur continued. "She urged me to return the fabric to Portland. She is a fascinating woman. I never thought I would actually meet an immortal."

Dan glanced in the rearview mirror. "The subpoena didn't get you here?"

"It was the instigation, yes, but not the deciding factor, Mr. Brick."

"Why didn't you tell me what was going on when we first talked, Spence? You too, Jean." Dan gripped the steering wheel.

"Would you have believed us?" Spence asked. "You were in a

different mindset before you witnessed the magic for yourself."

Dan went quiet.

"You can't understand until you've experienced the power of that fabric for yourself," Jean added. "Changes your view of everything."

"The birds still gone?" Dan asked.

"Yes, Agent Brick, and will remain so until the phoenixes take the next soul into immortality." Anhur smoothed the leather bundle in his lap. "You may want to consider..." His pause filled the car's interior with the hum of the tires.

"Consider what?"

"That...Mr. Flanders may not be the phoenixes' intended charge. A possibility."

Spence turned from the front seat. "He had to be. Legs made a conscious choice. If he'd let Brick set his hands on him, Legs would be immortal right now."

"Perhaps. Much of what was displayed last night revealed our ignorance. There is much we do not understand."

Jean's stomach knotted. Consideration of any other option never entered her mind. She leaned forward and gripped Spence's shoulder. "What did Dillon say when you called him?"

"He's going to the house. He'll stay until we get home. I told him to call if anything was up."

"Okay..."

"Don't worry," Spence assured and checked his cell phone. The low battery icon glowed orange. "Doc will look out for Dillon— maybe Birdie and Jess too." He opened his voice mail and held the screen up to Jean. "See? No messages."

The knot turned to a rock as Jean leaned back in the seat. "Dan, can you step on it? You won't get stopped."

"Hey! I'm starving. Remember?" Wheezy chided. "Let's go to the same place near Polyps."

"Puyallup," Dan corrected. "We're about five minutes away."

Wheezy held the harmonica to his mouth and whispered, "You

hungry, Legs?"

After dropping Anhur at the hotel at about eight in the morning, Spence gave Brick directions to their house. Physical and emotional exhaustion had settled over Wheezy as they passed through Vancouver into Oregon. His head floated like a buoy between Anhur's and Jean's shoulders.

As Dan turned the corner of their street, Jean blew out a breath. Interior lights illuminated the triangle-shaped windows above the dining room. Dillon being there filled Jean with relief.

"Come in, Dan," Jean said as they pulled into the driveway. "Wheezy's going to crash. Put your feet up on the couch. I don't want you to be alone right now. Plus, you must be exhausted."

"Just for a little while. Got any coffee?"

"Hot java coming up." She gave Wheezy a gentle poke. "C'mon, you. There's a bed with your name on it."

Wheezy stirred and yawned. Spence closed the trunk and carried their bags to the house. Brick helped Jean lift him out of the car.

"I can do it," he grouched. "Put me down, G-man."

Still asleep on his feet, Jean helped Wheezy teeter up the steps. As Spence moved to stick the key in the door, it opened as if by itself. Dillon stood in the entryway in a white terry cloth bathrobe. Tears streamed down his face. He raked his fingers through his long brown hair.

"What is it, honey?" Jean pushed past Spence. She reached out and drew Dillon in her arms. He pulled away. His young angel eyes gazed at her, pleading and with a pain she'd never seen before.

"Mycroft. He wouldn't eat. Wouldn't drink. I took him to bed with me after I got here around eleven. Wiley woke me up whining at about five thirty." Dillon choked on his words. "Mycroft wasn't acting right...too lethargic. So I took him to the emergency vet about two hours ago."

"Why didn't you call?"

"I did. I left messages on Spence's phone."

Spence checked his cell. "Dammit! Drained."

"They can't do anything. Cardiomyopathy. Heart disease. The vet said it's common there aren't any warning signs. Because of his age, they wanted to euthanize him. I told them no and brought him home." Dillon sobbed in Jean's arms.

"Where's Mycroft now?" She held his shoulders, forcing eye contact.

"I put him on your bed. Wiley's with him."

Jean raced up the stairs, followed by Spence. When she reached their bedroom, she stopped in the doorway. Mycroft was stretched out on a Pendleton wool blanket. Wiley licked his head in an attempt to heal. She lay down next to them both.

"What, baby?" She stroked Mycroft's long torso. His third eyelid rose at her touch. Spence sat on the bed next to her.

"He can't decide, Spence. We have to," Jean pleaded, her eyes desperate. The silent words that followed were not only understood but shared.

"I'll get Brick." Spence bolted from the room.

Jean reached out to Wiley's face and stroked his muzzle. "You want your Mycroft forever, don't you?"

Wiley dragged his tongue over her hand, tiny lights cascading through her fingers. He released a whine that peeled her insides and rested his head on the blanket. Warm brown eyes begged her with an endless gaze.

Memorizing every detail of Mycroft's living face, Jean released her denial. Gray would now blur the sharp definition of his cinnamon markings. His purr of distress, not pleasure, signaled time was short.

The squeak of the stairs gave her a start. Jean turned, unaware she'd been crying. Dan stood in the doorway, with Dillon, Spence, and Wheezy lined up behind him.

"Your hands. *Please*."

Dan's eyes appeared worn out, probably no different than hers. Spence sat next to her and stroked the cat's back.

"He's going to do it, honey. We talked downstairs."

With tentative steps, Dan moved forward. Jean grasped his hands and guided them, one on Mycroft's head between his ears, the other on his haunches.

"Meet Mycroft. He's the love of our lives. Don't you have someone special too, Dan? I bet you do."

"I did. Yes, I did."

Dan's face registered another world, one devoid of suspicion, skepticism, and doubt. He worked his fingers into the cat's fur.

"Something's...happening," he whispered. His chest heaved as it filled with air.

Spence stepped to the sliding glass door and glided it wide. A silent moment passed as the cool, early-morning breeze circled the room. Dillon led Wheezy toward the balcony outside. The three phoenixes materialized on the rail and gazed into the bedroom. They had been for Mycroft, all along. The background trills of the other birds in the trees went quiet. The air went quiet.

Long tail feathers in fiery hues of red and tangerine hung over the rungs, nearly touching the wood slats of the patio. Wheezy reached out and stroked the red crown of one of the three birds; Dillon held out his forefinger to the beak of another. One launched, followed by the second, and then the third. Wheezy raised his hand in a motionless wave, as if sending Legs with the phoenixes on their path beyond the trees. The morning air was still, except for the rush of thick wings.

Jean set her hand over Dan's. He opened his eyes and smiled with wonder.

Mycroft's image raised its head and gazed at each of them in a ghostly haze. He extended a paw toward Wiley, a smoky wake marking its path.

Dillon and Wheezy rushed from the balcony. They stood, gaping at Mycroft's image prancing around the blanket. Two cats: one lifeless, one alive. Dan reached out to pet the immortal cat, his own hand outlined as Mycroft pressed his head against his palm. A gesture of thanks.

A spray of sparkles swirled as both immortal animals jumped off the bed and raced toward the stairs. Wheezy dashed after them to follow.

"You did it," Jean whispered, her eyes locking on Dan's. "Anhur was right."

Dan embraced her, not a casual, distant gesture but a warm, genuine one. She figured it had been a long time since he'd allowed the magic of a hug in his life. A subtle woodsy scent—sweet cedar and lavender—released from his shirt. Less official than she had expected. She inhaled to forever associate the aroma with Mycroft's release into immortality.

"What's your scent?" Jean pulled away and searched his eyes.

"Potpourri. Hangs in my closet. My ex put it there. I never could bring myself to take it out. Scent is a comfort I can't explain."

"What's her name?"

"Christine." The way he said the name was like naming a new variety of rose, petals unfurling in a hue of soft peach.

"Keep it always." Jean patted his broad shoulder. "You have no idea how happy you've made Spence and me."

"And Doc," Spence said, shaking Dan's hand.

"Do you feel different...inside?"

"I'll never forget the experience...or all of you," Dan said.

"What are you going to do now with what you know?"

"The investigation is over, if that's what you mean. The first thing I'm doing, after you give me a cup of coffee, is to make a phone call to the woman I let walk away from me a year ago."

"Christine?" Jean asked.

Dan nodded.

"Good man," Spence declared.

Stretched out next to the former Mycroft, Dillon turned over his hand. He showed her Mycroft's favorite comb, the one with the tortoiseshell handle.

"Can I have some of his tail fur?" he asked. "I know it sounds weird, and a bit inappropriate, but I want to make a special set of brushes. They'll bear his name."

"Of course. The real Mycroft is downstairs," Jean said. "Speaking of painting portraits, I'm going down to check on Doc. He must be thrilled."

"Mycroft's probably tearing it up down there with Wiley."

Jean glanced at Mycroft's former self, lying lifeless on the blanket. Seventeen years of loyalty and love in one form and now thousands more in another.

"Is it a coincidence that Wiley was the same age when he became immortal too?" Spence said. His gaze followed the comb as Dillon made long strokes down the cat's torso to the end of his tail.

"Not a coincidence, I think."

"Choices, Jean," Dan said. "We make choices in the face of circumstances."

Led by Jean, the three of them streamed downstairs, leaving Dillon to his own immortalizing magic. Jean suspected he wanted privacy to comb Mycroft's fur.

"Where did they go?" she asked, her gaze sweeping the kitchen and entryway. Spence stepped to the living room and stood in front of Doc's portrait, the canvas that had so fascinated Legs.

"Found them!" he said, pointing. Spence turned, beaming.

Mycroft gazed at the group from Doc's lap. Wiley sat next to him with an expression more content than Jean had ever seen.

Doc winked and raised his forefinger to his bushy brow in a mock salute.

Openmouthed, Dan stood at the portrait. "Wha—? He's—"

Jean patted his arm. "Oh, it gets better. You're in for a ride, my friend." She stepped to the kitchen and picked up the phone. Scrolling through the recent inbound numbers, she pressed the one for the Hyatt Place Hotel.

"Good morning, Jean," Anhur answered, as if he'd been waiting for her call.

"How did you know?"

"Animals, too, have a soul. In many ways, they are more pure and noble than humans. That is why they were so revered by the ancients."

With his words, Jean envisioned the array of hieroglyphs in Nefertari's tomb: cats, horses, hawks, rams. All had been positioned more prominently than human forms.

"Check the fabric, Anhur. *Please.*"

She waited as the airwaves went silent, her heart pounding in her chest. The phone rustled as he came back on the line.

"The three phoenixes have returned."

Jean closed her eyes as the words registered. "Thank you, Anhur. We'll arrange a meeting at the museum on Monday. We all need a day of rest."

Jean set the phone in the charging stand, her throat burning. She and Spence needed to do more to deserve this gift. Accomplishments shouldn't be measured in dollars but in benevolence, respect. She raised her eyes to Dillon as he came down the stairs with a fluffy mound of ginger and cinnamon fur in his hand. She handed him a plastic bag. With infinite patience and commitment, he would thread each strand, one soft hair at a time, to create art—spectacular art.

Dan and Spence stood in front of Doc's portrait. She joined them. All of the subjects were now immortal. The canvas had a life all its own.

"Dillon is an unbelievable artist, by the way. This should be hanging in a museum." Dan leaned forward to inspect the brush strokes. "I can't believe it, but I'm looking right at him. The cat's in there," Dan shook his head.

"He'll come out when he's ready," Spence said. "Personality doesn't change with immortality."

All three of them stopped and looked at each other.

"What's that noise?" Brick asked, gazing around the living room.

"Where's Wheezy?" Jean hadn't seen him since coming downstairs.

Spence turned and elbowed her. "Check this out."

Behind them, Wheezy had his feet up on the hassock with his head back on the couch. His wingtips had been tossed on the floor. With his mouth open wide, Wheezy sucked in air with a long snore.

"Poor guy. He's exhausted."

"Should we let him stay there and just put a blanket over him?"

"No, I think he needs a good night sleep. I don't want him to wake up and try to go up the stairs while he's really tired. He hates the stairs."

Brick chuckled. "I'll carry him up." Dan lifted Wheezy in his arms, his glasses askew and black socks bouncing with each step up the stairs toward the guest room. Dan turned on the landing. "Damn, he's heavy."

CHAPTER 23

The Chief Needs a Vacation

On Monday morning in the FBI offices, Jon Segert stared at Dan on the other side of his desk. For the past twenty minutes, he'd been listening to Brick debrief him on the weekend's events. He'd never seen anyone alter their view of life in only forty-eight hours. Experience told him that people couldn't change the color of their inner stripes—but Brick had indeed changed his.

"Seems like you understand more about this stuff than I do."

"I'm a novice. I don't think even Anhur Kumar's got all the answers." Brick pumped his fingers as if performing a physical therapy exercise.

"I've seen some things, Dan, but I didn't go through the process of making anyone immortal." Jon wasn't prepared for the sudden attack of jealousy. Until now, the knowledge had been secret, shared only by a handful of people in the world. "What was the experience like?" He leaned forward on his elbows. Even Brick's face seemed different—relaxed, hopeful.

"Amazing. And not just physically either. I spent all of yesterday thinking I've wasted so much time on things that don't matter. When that cat got up with his body lying on the bed, something happened to me inside—rearranged my organs."

"Rearranged your priorities, you mean." Jon jutted his chin at Brick's hands. "Still tingling?"

"Sometimes. Got a weird vision this morning when I put on this old wristwatch. Belonged to my grandfather. I inherited it." Brick's expression became playful. He glanced at the Roman numerals on the mother-of-pearl face. The band was made of alligator skin, shiny from wear.

"See more than you bargained for?"

"Mmm-hmm. You could say that. The man went to church every Sunday, but I didn't know he was into porn," Brick laughed. "The Collinses and Kumar are right. We can't talk about this to anyone. So, Doc said he helped you solve the Dromov case."

"Jess did too."

Brick leaned forward. "How?"

"Can you believe they're both over a hundred and forty years old. Jess helped me get to Winthrop, and Doc helped me solve the Dromov case with this painting by bidding against Dromov." Jon turned and pointed to *The Dancing Boy* above his desk. "Originally belonged to Doc."

Brick fixed on the painting, incredulous, but then his expression went studious. "Wait a minute! I recognize the style...but something's off. Who painted it?"

"Caravaggio and a guy named Brugghen. This is the painting that helped me bring down Dromov. The Collinses inherited it. Caused quite a stir at the auction in London."

"You serious? Hendrick ter Brugghen?"

Jon blinked at Brick. He had no idea Dan knew anything about art. The man was full of surprises this morning.

"I'm impressed."

"Yeah. He was Dutch," Dan continued. "Part of the Caravaggisti around 1610. Pretty rare, Jon." He stood for a closer scrutiny of the canvas. "What are you thinking by having this in the office?" Brick stepped to the small portrait in its ornate gold-leaf frame. He inspected the details of the cherubic features of the young boy dancing in a clearing in the woods. "This painting should be in a museum."

"Want to blow your hair back? I bet you're still full of magic. Set your hand on the canvas."

With no hesitation, Dan set his hand on the image. Golden light erupted and streamed through Brick's fingers. He closed his eyes and arched his eyebrows as the beams boiled, soundless and without heat. Dan's forehead wrinkled, as if in pain. He lifted his hand. The light stopped.

"I'll be damned. I had no idea—and I studied art history in college."

"What did you see?"

"Caravaggio really did turn Tommasoni into a eunuch before killing him."

Jon's fingers prickled as he grazed his hand over his stiff crew cut. "If anyone walked in here right now, we'd be suspended and put into counseling." Jon glanced at his watch. "Time to go in the penalty box. The chief wants an update from *both* of us."

"This ought to be fun."

"Can you believe I showed him the talon a couple of months ago?" Jon hesitated as he held the handle of his office door. "I'm sorry I don't have Horus anymore. Pretty handy in an interrogation."

"Did the claw actually transform into a hawk?"

"Sure did. Bit the hell out of Dromov. Cried like a baby."

"Gotta get me one those, my friend." Dan slapped Jon on the back.

Jon glanced at Brick as he rapped on the chief's open door. This time he was actually looking forward to meeting with the man. The two agents stepped inside the office and stood side-by-side in front of the desk. A picture had been added to the credenza behind the chief: the chief with his two chins holding a slab of ribs in long tongs over a smoking gas grill. The slogan on his T-shirt said, *I Got Your Vegan.*

"Sit!" the chief ordered, pointing to the chairs. He never raised his eyes from the report in front of him.

Jon sat, followed by Brick, and craned his neck to glimpse what the chief had in front of him. The words *Enzer Pharmaceuticals* and *hawk* popped from the paper.

"Should I give you two commendations or suspensions?" One of the chief's chins bulged over his white collar. "I know Jon was working on Forrester and Hughes in Seattle — nice work, by the way — but what were you doing up there, Brick? Fishin' with the Pharaoh?"

"Separate investigation, sir," Brick said and smirked at Jon. "Anhur Kumar. He's one of the most honorable men I've ever met."

"Other than me, right? You gotta let this hawk thing go. You're obsessed."

"Consider the matter closed."

The chief narrowed his eyes inside two dark, baggy circles, distrustful of getting his way without a smackdown. "Is this the ooga-booga crap I heard about at Forrester's party?"

"What booga crap is that, Chief?" Jon asked, inspecting his fingernails. "Got a clipper on you, Brick?"

"Shooting lights! Flying fire! Blue lightning!" Witnesses said there was an explosion with a hawk in flames!" He tapped his pen on his desk and studied the two men. "Again with the damned hawk. Something funny went on up there."

"Special effects. Forrester spent a bundle on fireworks," Brick offered.

The chief scrunched his face until he resembled a dried-apple doll from a curiosity shop. He pressed his lips together and pushed a rush of air out of his nose like a taunted bull.

"Getting nowhere fast on this one." The chief took off his half-moon glasses and rubbed his eyelids. "Sorry about Flanders. Quite a loss. We should all be so lucky to make eighty-two. Went out doing what he loved." His iridescent-green eyes softened. "Do you know I have three albums he and Beevers played on?" From his expression, the chief was getting ready to launch into old concert stories.

"A big loss," Jon agreed. "I'd grown attached to Legs. Wheezy's still in Portland, if you want to get your records signed. You want to meet him?"

"Yeah. I think I would. Where's Nash Winthrop? That weasel skip town?"

"Staying low until he's called to testify. He's cooperating. In fact, he won't stop calling me about the trial date. I told him to keep Kip's check as compensation. It'll keep him in rent for awhile. The recording of Forrester and Hughes is irrefutable evidence. Slam dunk."

"What happened to Forrester's goddamned nose? He's been moaning about his honker for two days. Why are all your perps whiners, Segert?"

"Wheezy Beevers, sir. Coldcocked him over the harmonica."

"Well, good! Finally, somebody in this case has some old-fashioned kahunas. And the guy can play a helluva piano too."

"Those would be *cojones*, sir," Brick corrected. "He's got spunk."

"Whatever they are, I hope a conviction scares the hell out of anybody even thinking about leaking information. Made me watch my own mouth, I tell you." The chief laughed louder than was warranted.

"Doubtful," Jon quipped.

The chief grimaced. "You watch your mouth too."

Jon recovered, figuring he'd pushed too hard. "These guys are ants in the desert. For every mound you find, there are thousands underground."

"I believe that's called job security, Jon." The chief turned to Brick. "So, were the Collinses accessories in Raleigh Coulter's death or not?"

"No evidence to suggest they were involved," Brick hedged. "They were extremely cooperative. The whole incident in London was an accident."

"The report stands, then? A brain hemorrhage—in his *thigh*?"

"From what I found out about Coulter, sir, he probably had more intellectual activity going on in that body part."

Jon raised the knuckle of his forefinger to his lips to hide a laugh. Brick was getting good at this brief-with-the-chief stuff.

"Not helpful, Dan. Won't fly." The chief pointed at Jon. "Where's the goddamned claw—that crazy talon thingy you showed me a while back? I wanna use it to shave the smug grin off your face."

"What talon thingy, sir?" Jon shrugged and turned to Brick. "You got a crazy talon thingy?"

Brick shook his head. "Not me. You need a vacation, Chief."

"Yeah. Take your wife to Richmond, Virginia," Jon suggested. "The Old Gaines House would be a relaxing getaway. I'll hook you up."

"Get the hell out of here—both of you! I got your vacation."

CHAPTER 24

Bottom Up. Top Down.

At ten o'clock on Monday morning, Jean heard the shower shut off in the guest bathroom. She retrieved a second mug and filled it with coffee, two sugars, and a splash of half-and-half. Wheezy descended the stairs in a red cotton bathrobe. His rounded image made her smile: a giant Nerf ball with black glasses. The comb-over wisp had already dried.

"Mornin'!" she said and set the mug on the kitchen island for Wheezy.

"Where is everybody?" Wheezy yawned and shook his head like a hairless dog being doused with a hose.

"You needed the rest. It's been a wild and emotional week. Spence is downtown at the museum with Anhur, making arrangements for the fabric to be exhibited. Anhur leaves tomorrow. Then, Spence will be at the store this afternoon with Bill. I have no idea where Mycroft and Wiley got off to. They were here earlier."

"I'm glad those birds are staying here."

Jean took a sip of her black coffee, eyeing Wheezy over the rim of the mug. She waited for clarification of the statement.

"I'm just sayin'." Wheezy raised his hands in defense. "Don't read anything into that."

"You and I need to go to the funeral home and fill out some paperwork for Legs. His body will arrive there tomorrow. Are you up to it?"

"Yeah, no choice. He wanted me to handle the details. We had a pact. If I went first, he would've made arrangements for me. We left each other everything in our wills." Wheezy rolled his eyes. "Crap! Another thing I gotta do." He pointed to Jean's ever-ready list. This one had two columns: one for her and one for Wheezy. "Write that down on mine: call lawyer to change will."

Jean rummaged for a pen in the drawer and added the task to the already long list. The printed slogan on the top of the pad read, *Cats Take Messages and Get Back to You Later.*

"Do you have all the information you need?"

"I got his wallet and copies of papers in my suitcase. At our age, it's not a good idea to travel without docs. Will you and Spence take care of arrangements for me when the time comes?"

Wheezy asked the question so casually. Arrangements.

"Of course…whichever road you choose. Plenty of living to do, though. Why don't you stay in Portland? We'll help you move."

Wheezy's face brightened as he warmed to the idea. "Where would I live? Not with you. I'd drive you nuts." He tightened the belt on his robe. "I'm mighty particular in my ways."

"I hadn't noticed," she quipped. "Seriously, though, we inherited Mary Coulter's bungalow in northeast Portland. Only ten minutes away. Beautiful neighborhood. The renovation is almost done. Want to move in?"

"Not for free. I'll pay the going rent."

"Deal. We'll drop by the house after we leave the funeral home. I'll show you around. The painters might be there. I need to check on their progress, anyway."

"Stairs?"

"Yes, but you need the exercise."

"You're cruel, Wicked Witch of the West. I'll get dressed; you make breakfast. Two eggs over easy and toast…lots of butter." Wheezy turned and held his robe closed as he bolted up the stairs.

Jean hadn't seen him climb those steps that fast before. *Faker.*

Helping Wheezy through the details of Legs's death had been tough. Jean had a difficult time with the process of reducing a legend to fill-in boxes on a form. No space had been allocated to record him as loyal friend, confidant, musical genius, and inspiration to others. The funeral director had been patient and empathetic. He'd even heard of Legs, whose ashes could be picked up in a couple of weeks. They'd wait for the call once the artist completed the custom etching on the urn.

The walk was quiet as Jean ushered Wheezy to the T-Bird in the parking lot.

"I hate funeral homes," Wheezy declared as he plopped in the passenger seat and struggled to buckle the seat belt.

"You sure you don't want even a small memorial service for Legs?" Jean couldn't help but check once more.

"Legs was adamant on that point, Jean. He hated the thought of anyone sniveling or crying about him. "He told me—just like this—'Tell 'em to go put one-a my records on the spinner and take a shot of tequila. Turn it up real loud.'" Wheezy tried to make his high-pitched voice sound like Legs's deep one. He sucked in a breath. "But it's a beautiful day, in spite of the crappy situation."

"You're a trouper, Wheezy. The urn you picked out is perfect. The musical notes around the top will be a nice touch." Wheezy had taken ten minutes to sketch out a phrase from "I'm Ready" for the funeral director to give to the artist.

"Not just a pretty face, Jean. I got it *all* going on." Wheezy pressed his lips together and snapped his fingers in rhythm. "Taste and style."

"No argument from me, darlin'," Jean said, peering over her black sunglasses. She pulled on her driving gloves and started the engine. "Let's go see your new home. Rent or buy—doesn't matter to Spence and me."

"Ugh. I'm dreading the move. Two lifetimes' worth of stuff.

Remember, we need to deal with Legs's townhouse too."

"One step at a time. I'll hire a good real estate agent in DC first. Then, they'll work with the moving company to get everything packed up and put in a van."

"Oh no, I'm not putting my Bösendorfer in a moving van. White gloves only."

"The *Baby*dorfer can come out first, with a professional piano mover."

"What about selling both places?"

"Once the townhouses are empty, they'll hire a cleaning crew. After that, both of them can be staged with rental furniture. The costs will be taken from the proceeds when the houses are sold. And, lo and behold, ten days later your and Legs's stuff will be here. We'll overnight the keys so you don't have to travel anywhere. All will be done through e-mail and on the phone."

Wheezy's shoulders relaxed. "Okay. What the hell. So, I just bark orders to you, and it all gets done?"

"Yep."

"You'll be my secretary!"

"I prefer *personal assistant*. Yes, I'll make the arrangements." Jean already had a checklist scrolling through her head.

"I think you're going to love Mary's bungalow. There are plenty of other options, though. I should have gone into real estate, but I didn't want to deal with difficult people." She glanced at him and smirked.

"What? I'm easy!"

"Uh-huh."

"Wait! Stop the car!" Wheezy shouted. "This is a convertible. Open her up!"

Jean pulled into a shady corner of a bank parking lot. She hit the switch to lower the top. Over the mechanical whir, she said: "We might have company. Wiley never misses a ride when the top's down."

"Can everybody see him?"

"No idea. Probably not."

Jean and Wheezy stared at each other, waiting. She broke her gaze and turned when Wiley appeared with his paws up on the seat back, followed by Mycroft. He, too, stood on his hind feet, gazing over the trunk.

"Paws inside, everybody. That includes you, Wheezy."

As Jean drove up McLoughlin Avenue toward Irvington, they laughed at the sparkles flying off both tails. Mycroft's stretched out straight and fluttered in the breeze. The neighborhood changed to become a shady canopy of old-growth trees as they turned on Knott Street. She relayed her and Spence's history of living two blocks away from Mary in the early nineties.

"Spence and I used to jog past Mary's house. We'd see her cleaning out her bird bath in the morning. She's a lovely woman, Wheezy. I think you'll like her."

"I sure like the neighborhood so far," Wheezy said as they turned on Nineteenth Street. Flickers of sunlight sparkled on his glasses as he admired the quiet street of bungalows, Cape Cods, and Foursquares from the twenties. Each one was unique and had its own architectural character. Jean had decided to have Mary's house painted a sunny yellow with bright white trim. With the wide porch and two eyebrow dormer windows on the second floor, the house resembled a smiling face.

"Here we are. I don't see the painters' truck. Must be on a lunch break. We'll have the house to ourselves. Jean pulled into the steep driveway and turned off the engine. "You'll be living in an immortal woman's house, Wheezy. Are you okay with that? Mary could pop in on you."

"What am I going to do, rattle around in there all by myself?"

"Duly noted. Let's go in."

Wiley and Mycroft jumped out of the car and ran ahead to the front door. Impatient, they disappeared inside.

"Steps. I hate you, woman."

"You'll thank me later." Jean helped Wheezy climb to the porch.

New thick chains on the wood-slat swing, intended for two, hung from the deep overhang. "You need the exercise. No Voodoo Doughnuts for you, mister. Do you have a car?"

"I'll get a smart car. This is Portland. I don't want to get egged by the bark eaters for buying a Suburban."

"You wouldn't be able to see over the steering wheel, anyway."

Jean turned the brass key in the freshly varnished oak door. The Craftsman pattern of the panels only hinted at the striking details inside. A waft of fresh acrylic hit her in the face. Sheets covered the refinished antique oak floors.

"Let's keep the door open to air out these fumes."

Wheezy followed her inside, his gaze arcing to take in the original amber-glass light fixtures, tapered pillars on the low room divider, rippled glass, and dental crown molding. He was drawn to the cozy sitting area off the entryway, flanked by bookcases. The space was only big enough for two chairs in front of the small fireplace. He turned in a circle with his arms spread.

"Here's where I'm going to read. Good for cold, rainy nights."

Jean breathed in silent relief. Wheezy liked it.

The fresh paint on the first floor reflected a buttery toffee with shiny white trim. The outside cheer had been carried inside, only in a warmer and more intimate hue.

"Do you have a lot of furniture, Wheezy?"

"Not much, but my piano will take up half the living room. We'll do concert night on Sundays. I hate my furniture, anyway. Top of the line seventies."

"Sounds like a plan."

Wheezy swished across the sheets to the kitchen. The original laminate countertops had been updated to neutral chocolate-veined granite. He ran his fingers over the reflective surface.

"Nice. I'm glad you kept the old O'Keefe & Merritt. Rosey cooked for Legs on one of these for years." He turned and chuckled. "What's with the blue rotary phone?"

"Original to the house." Jean picked up the receiver and handed it to Wheezy. "Unfortunately, it doesn't work, but I had an experience with this phone after we made Mary Coulter immortal. I didn't have the heart to get rid of it."

"Hello? Hello?" Wheezy pretended someone was on the line. "Oh hi, Mary! Tonight? I don't know—you'll have to check with my *secretary.*" He opened his mouth in a silent laugh and pointed to Jean.

Jean rolled her eyes. "Hang up, Wheez—" A ripple in her peripheral vision drew her gaze to the refrigerator. The air in front of the stainless steel blurred the word *Frigidaire* in the top right corner.

Wheezy stepped forward and waved his hand against the heated current. "What's that? Paint fumes?"

"Mary?" Jean whispered, searching for a form to appear. An image strengthened until Mary stood in front of them.

"Hello, dear. A lovely transformation of the house." Mary turned and extended her hand to Wheezy. "I'm afraid we haven't been introduced."

As if in a trance, Wheezy stared at Mary, inspecting the hazy outline illuminating her face and hand.

"This is Wheezy Beevers. He's going to live in your house," Jean said, embracing her. "And this, Wheezy, is the illustrious Mary Coulter."

In silence, Wheezy wrapped his fingers around Mary's. He turned them over and kissed her knuckles. His magnified eyes gazed at her in awe. Blooms of pink appeared on Mary's cheeks.

"And fill your home with music," he cooed. "I am honored to be given the opportunity."

"Oh, Mr. Beevers, the privilege is mine. May I show you the house?"

"Nothing would make me happier." He looped his arm over hers and turned back to Jean. "Cancel all my appointments for the rest of the day."

Resting her head against the jamb of the kitchen doorway, Jean studied the pair as they strolled through the living and dining rooms. Mycroft raced by their feet and padded up the stairs, followed by

Wiley's clattering toenails on the wood steps. Mary relayed her decorating suggestions and talked of holidays gone by. The expression on each of their faces signaled the chemistry that was percolating. She wished Legs were still here to witness the scene. But this moment belonged to Wheezy…and Mary.

"This is where you might set up the Christmas tree," Mary suggested, her small voice echoing around the room, "full of heirloom ornaments." She stood at the front window, framed by panes of sparkling glass. "You do know, the freshest trees come from this area, Mr. Beevers."

"Right. No fake ones. Should be illegal," Wheezy agreed. "I'll have Jean go out and chop one down immediately."

Mary led Wheezy to the sitting area where she'd relaxed in the evening with her husband, Jim. He read his mystery novels; she worked on her embroidery.

Wheezy ran his hand over the polished oak bookshelves. "If I put two comfortable chairs here, will you sit with me at night while I dive into a good book?" He practically crooned as he gazed into Mary's honey-flecked hazel eyes. She was smitten too. Jean couldn't believe Mary was buying his Valentino act.

"I *will*. This is my favorite part of the house," she declared and let out a sigh. "What do you like to read, Mr. Beevers?"

"Call me Franklin." Jean startled at his suggestion. Wheezy was growing up. "I can't get enough mysteries, especially Raymond Chandler. He writes good bad guys."

Mary squeezed his arm. "We're going to be dear friends, Franklin."

"When my piano gets here, I'll play you some Debussy that'll skip your immortal heart." He gave Mary a peck on her cheek. Wheezy turned back to Jean and winked. "Forget the rent. I'm buying the place—cash."

CHAPTER 25

Alliances

On Tuesday afternoon, nearly one week after his arrival in Portland, Anhur prepared to return to Cairo. The board of the Portland Museum of Art had wholeheartedly agreed to be caretakers of the fabric for an indefinite period of time. They all hoped it could return to its home eventually, but no one could predict how long the protests in Egypt would last, or to what level they'd escalate. Maybe the grand affair in Cairo that Jean had fantasized about would happen someday, but not someday soon. For now there was no fancy dinner, cocktails, and speeches to extol the virtues of generosity, only a deal for something more important. The fabric—and its secrets—would remain safe.

The engines of the jet whined outside the terminal door. Anhur held out his hands to her, Spence, Jon, and Dan.

"I must go. Yet again, an adventure beyond comprehension."

"The museum will be excellent stewards of the fabric," Spence assured. "This will open up all kinds of possibilities. The board is thrilled with the new relationship."

"Yes, I have much to do in the coming months. A comprehensive traveling exhibit of items from Nefertari's tomb will take much coordination with the other museums that house its artifacts."

"Quite the coup for Portland," Jean added. "And you too, Anhur. Don't forget to get her sandals from that museum in Torino,

Italy."

"And the Senet set from the Brooklyn Museum," Spence added.

"No, do not worry. I do remember your enthusiasm about those items in particular."

Dan stepped forward and embraced Anhur as an old friend.

"You and that fabric changed my life," he said.

"Mr. Brick, it is not what objects can do but the actions you take from their meaning. Thank you for pushing me to bring it here. I believe the artifact is now safe."

"Well, I'm a different man than I was last week, before you arrived. Quite the experience."

"You should consider yourself quite privileged. Cats are manifestations of gods in my culture. You made an earthly one immortal."

Dan blinked, digesting Anhur's words. Jon stepped behind him.

"C'mon, back to the office. I need your help to finish the trial prep on Forrester and Hughes." Jon leaned toward Anhur. "So, what happened to the talon? Will it reappear? I found Horus pretty handy."

"I can't say, Mr. Segert. The talon is reunited with the fabric. I don't believe you need Horus. He is inside of you." Anhur set his hand on Jon's shoulder. "Protect my friends until I return for the opening of the exhibition."

Anhur picked up his leather bag and stepped toward the door. He turned and hesitated, as if he wanted to say something more. He gave Jean a heartfelt smile, like he didn't want to leave. "Be well. I am looking forward to finally having our celebration."

The engine noise obliterated any further conversation when he opened the glass door. Jean's gaze followed him out to the tarmac. He climbed the stairs, gave them one final wave, and disappeared. She checked her watch and turned to Spence.

"Time to do good things. Off to Landrum & Sullivan to become immortal."

"Yep. Don Landrum is waiting. Let's go." Spence took her hand and followed Dan and Jon through the terminal.

The studio at the Northwest Institute of Art was quiet during the week. Classrooms here were made for introspection and creative exploration. Individual studios, in particular, were birthing rooms for imagination channeled through paint.

A couple of hours remained before Dillon's next class, which gave him plenty of time to check on the drying process. He sat on the stool and pulled back the sheet from the canvas. The thinnest needle from a set of four held the verdict. A slight poke to the surface of Mary's lip. No. Not yet.

Four, maybe five, weeks remained before Wheezy moved into Mary's house. While her portrait dried, Dillon would start on Mycroft. The pencil sketch of the cat reaching out to the three phoenixes in flight needed a bit more work. He'd use the singular line of Mycroft brushes to create their namesake.

A whisk of his finger over his cell phone produced the photo Dillon had used as his guide for the portrait in front of him: Mary Coulter sitting on the edge of his bed, Wiley stretched across her lap, when he, Jean, and Spence visited the Richmond house in the spring. The night Doc had given him back his hearing. Mary had appeared to him with Wiley, and in those few minutes, Dillon had become fascinated by her. So much so that he was compelled to replicate her immortality in oil. Something about her—words couldn't articulate her grace in the same rhythm as paint would. He set the phone on the easel next to the canvas.

Adjusting the swing-arm lamp over the face, Dillon inspected the illuminated fine lines around Mary's hazel eyes, results of her slight smile as she gazed up at *The Dancing Boy* on the wall.

"Oh, Dillon. Is this me?" Mary's voice came behind him. The purity of its humble timbre filled him with life, as if the woman had jumped from the canvas. He smiled but didn't turn.

"Yes, Mary. Exactly as you are."

Mary stepped forward and extended her hazy fingers. "Can I

touch?"

"Just Wiley's head. That part is completely dry. Odd how paint works—it only comes alive when it hardens, void of moisture. Opposite of life."

Dillon watched Mary reach out to the canvas. With pride he beamed at Mary's fascination of her immortal self. Hesitant, she lightly touched the dog's brow. Wiley blinked and licked her fingers. As soon as Mary lifted her hand away, the image stilled.

"Not in your pieces, Dillon. Yours are full of life, even when they're not dry."

"You have the touch."

"So do you. Like Caravaggio. Real."

"When does Wheezy move into the house?" Dillon asked, inspecting one of the Mycroft brushes. This one had been perfect for replicating the wispy outline around Mary's gray and chestnut hair pulled back in a twist.

"Four weeks and two days," she whispered.

Dillon turned to her with a knowing smile from behind the curtain of his dark, silky locks. He was thrilled that she had found the second love in her life.

Mary blushed. A sanguine expression lit up her face as she held out her fingers to inspect his brush.

"But who's counting, right?" he said, handing it to her. "You want to give this portrait to him?"

"You do it, Dillon. From you, not me." Mary poked his shoulder with the bottom end of the brush, and his skin tingled beneath his cotton shirt. "Do you have time to paint one more?"

Dillon raised his eyes. "Who?"

Mary ran the soft bristles over her cheek. Her eyelids lowered as if the cat's hair contained a soul and was communicating with her.

"A surprise for Wheezy to hang over his piano. It would mean so much to him."

"Don't tell me..." Dillon reached for his phone. The gallery of stored photos held several options. Instinct drew him to one particular image as his fingertip swished through the search. He stopped, satisfied he'd found his prize, and showed the screen to Mary.

"How about this one?"

"Perfect."

CHAPTER 26

Movin' In

The dog days of August were a whirlwind of activity at the Irvington bungalow. Jean had gotten everything done but not without blips. Spence refereed a few sessions of he-said-she-said between Jean and Wheezy over misplaced keys and lost paperwork, but the scrappy moments always ended with peals of laughter. Both townhouses in the desirable Georgetown neighborhood in Washington, DC, had sold within one day of going on the market, which was a blessing and a curse. The quick sales turned their timeline into a Rubik's Cube of coordination.

At the last minute, Wheezy decided to donate his bigger pieces of furniture (an overstuffed Naugahyde couch, two matching chairs, and cantilevered chrome lamps from the seventies) in favor of new Stickley-style pieces to match the design of the house. He'd made Jean intercept the movers while in transit to request they stop at Goodwill to avoid loading and unloading those select items twice. In replacing the pieces, Jean chalked up the experience as one of her more entertaining shopping excursions. She called it the *bounce-bounce-aahhhh* test. Wheezy needed to assess the comfort and buoyancy of every option in the store. Her threat to tip him over in a recliner forced his decision to go with the oak-and-leather living room set.

The same qualities that made Wheezy a gifted musician earned him the reputation of being a terrible boss; compromise and patience weren't his greatest strengths. Without Legs's calm demeanor by his side, Wheezy's high-strung personality roared unchecked like a tsunami, and the delay in getting the Bösendorfer moved sent him spinning in the curl of the wave. Instead of being first, as promised, the piano was the caboose in the arrival of Wheezy's possessions.

But they enjoyed bright spots too. The closing on the Irvington house had taken all of fifteen minutes. Wheezy simply presented a check in full, signed his name to the paperwork (without reading any of it), and told the title officer at the bank they needed to make their reservation for an early dinner at Portofino, an intimate Italian restaurant in Sellwood. He was addicted to their homemade gnocchi with fresh Parmesan and truffle oil. Every milestone of the transition had to be punctuated with a meal—and her waistline suffered in the process.

"Here comes the piano, Wheezy!" Jean shouted. She stood at the front window as the truck pulled to the curb, brushing the low-hanging branches of the old growth maple. The words *Music in Motion* raced down the full length of its side. "This is the grand finale. Everything's here. You're officially a resident of Portlandia."

"Took long enough. It was supposed to be here *before* the moving van," Wheezy scoffed, his hands on his hips. "Where are Spence and Dillon? They need to help us unpack these boxes."

"No grumping. Didn't you get the memo?" She suspected his less-than-buoyant mood was prompted by Mary's conspicuous absence over the past two days.

"I'm going to fire you for insubordination."

"You're not getting off that easy. What the heck is going on with your outfit?" Jean started laughing.

"I got this when we went to the Saturday Market." He smoothed the globe under his long-sleeved navy-blue T-shirt. The sleeves were too long, but the slogan written on the front of his shirt stretched with strain: *You Should See My Bobblehead.*

"The fashion police will be arriving any minute. But Spence went to help Bill at the store this morning and is picking up Dillon. They'll be here a bit later," she said.

Wheezy shook his head and scanned the living and dining room. The stacks of boxes seemed daunting.

"I'm glad you told the movers not to take Legs's albums into storage." Jean pointed to five book boxes at the base of the stairs. "They deserve to be with you."

"We're not unpacking those," Wheezy said. "They belong down at the store with his hutch. I'm giving the records to Spence and Bill. They've got a shrine set up down there. I'll sign them as Legs's representative to give them some extra oomph."

"Make them a surprise. Tomorrow, we'll take a break from unpacking and drive them down to the store. They'll want to make a signing event of it."

Two movers in thick gloves climbed the steps with paperwork. She ushered them inside before they could knock.

"Wheezy? Tell these guys exactly how you want the piano positioned," she said, holding open the front door. A warm breeze circled the room, and a robin flew inside on the current. The bird landed on the mantle of the fireplace in the sitting area. With tentative steps, she approached the bird and cupped her hands around its broad tangerine chest.

"You're early," she whispered, imagining Mary had flown in. "Come back in an hour." Jean released the bird to the porch. It wasn't Mary, of course, but the possibility filled her with anticipation for the surprise Spence and Dillon had planned. She hoped Mary would make an appearance.

"Keyboard should face the front window at a forty-five degree angle. I want to see outside when I play," Wheezy instructed. He scrunched his eyes and pointed. "And be careful!"

"Not our first gig, sir. We'll bring in the legs first."

As the truck pulled away, Wheezy sat at the piano and ran his hands up the full length of the keyboard. He'd returned to his old self with ivory under his fingers. Jean clapped.

"Sounds pretty good after three thousand miles," Wheezy announced. He rubbed the Austrian spruce wood, appreciating the care the movers took to prevent a scratch in the finish.

"Play something!"

He rubbed his fingers together and pushed up his sleeves.

"Here's one for you." He dove into Billy Joel's "Movin' Out" and laughed.

"Billy Joel?"

"Movin' *in*, Jean!" he shouted. Wheezy started to sing, replacing the word in the lyrics.

Halfway through the song, his fingers slowed. After a moment of quiet, Debussy's "Clair de Lune" filled the living room. Mary appeared on the bench next to him. Jean's heart melted as Wheezy turned to her and beamed. Mary's timing couldn't have been more perfect.

"Lovely, Franklin," Mary said. "I could listen to this one forever."

"You just might," Wheezy said, never taking his gaze from her as he played.

Jean stepped to the window as she listened to the beautiful melody. A hint of a smile crossed her face as Spence's Mini Cooper pulled into the driveway. Lost in the lilting tune and Mary, Wheezy was in his own new world. Tiptoeing to the front door, Jean waved Spence and Dillon inside, each carrying a square package wrapped in brown paper. She put a finger to her lips.

All three of them stood in the living room and waited for Wheezy to finish the delicate cadence of his serenade to Mary. They gave him a round of applause. Wheezy spun around on the piano bench.

"What you got, Spence?" He rubbed his hands together.

"These are housewarming presents for you. Your walls need decoration, especially the one behind the piano."

Mary nodded, trying to hide her excitement, but her eyes shone with a twinkle. Wheezy hopped off the bench and stepped to the two-foot-by-three-foot package in Spence's hands. He pulled a corner. The ripped paper fell to the floor as his expression collapsed.

The portrait showed Legs hunched over his harmonica with squinted eyes, bathed in brilliant blue and gold light beams radiating from the mouthpiece. Lost in his music, he appeared unaware of its emotional affect on the crowd at the festival. Behind him to the left, Wheezy sat at the Steinway, mouth open in a silent laugh. His shoes were blurred with movement.

"A magic moment frozen in time," Jean said.

"Dillon captured him so well," Spence added. "I'll never forget that singular moment."

Dillon studied his sneakers, modest in relation to the enormity of his talent.

"For you, Wheezy," he said, his voice nearly a whisper.

"I...don't...have the words to even begin to tell you how special this is," Wheezy said, running his hand along the edge of the reflective bronzed frame.

"And this is too." Jean reached into her pocket and pulled out a silver coin. She turned to Dillon and took his hand. She set the coin in his palm. "This seems like the right time to give it to you. Legs gave this Indian Head nickel to me when we were at his house in DC. He wanted you to have it. This was the first nickel Legs ever saved, after his gig with Dizzy Gillespie and John Coltrane."

Dillon stared at his palm as if a lifetime were contained in the small talisman. The metal had warmed from being inside Jean's pocket. He didn't speak. He couldn't.

Wheezy composed himself and tore his gaze from the painting. "I remember that gig. Let me see." He plucked the coin from Dillon's hand. "Legs and I went to this bar next to the club. We had two shots of tequila. Legs spent all—almost all—his money on some perfume for Rosey...Joy, it was called. The only scent she ever wore. That nickel was what he had left. We played a game: 'If I had a nickel for every time...'" Wheezy imitated Legs's voice but couldn't continue when his words cracked. He stopped and handed the Indian Head back to Dillon, clearing his throat. "Now…I have a surprise for me too. I bought *myself* a piece of art. Be right back."

Jean gave Spence a quizzical shrug. "Did you do something sneaky?"

"Not me," Spence countered and turned to Dillon.

"Me neither. I have the other one here." Dillon bounced the wrapped portrait. "Mary?"

"No idea. Franklin didn't say a word to me."

Wheezy stepped into the living room with a small painting, showing only the back. The frame was familiar. He made a production of turning it around.

Jean sucked in a breath. "*The Dancing Boy*," she whispered. "How? When?"

"The G-man and I worked everything out," Wheezy crowed.

"Did he cut you a good deal?" Spence asked.

"A bargain at $750,000." Wheezy laughed and rocked the framed dancing image in his hands. "Better than giving my money to the government."

"But you did give your money to the government."

"Nope. The proceeds are going directly to Dromov's victims, not for lawyers' fees or buying gold-plated toilets seats," Wheezy declared. "G-man said you have a written agreement that stipulates how the funds are to be used."

"Well, I can't think of a more appropriate place for this painting, except for maybe the museum," Spence added.

"Art was never the same after Caravaggio," Dillon said. "A moment of transition in the world of genius. You and Legs did that with music too." Dillon turned with an expression of quiet respect for Wheezy's eighty-two years of wisdom. "Every generation of artists makes something that can't be replicated."

Jean couldn't think of anything to add, except maybe to request Dillon set his hand on the painting. But Dillon's profound words were enough. No light show or vision could say more.

"I bought well." Wheezy raised his misty eyes.

Mary stood next to him and stared at *The Dancing Boy* in disbelief. Having remained quiet, she broke the still moment. "Finally, it's come home. You have no idea the importance of what you've done, Franklin."

"What do you mean? I just wanted to make sure this painting didn't go to a stranger."

"You'll see." Mary stepped to Dillon and brushed his hair behind his shoulder. She gave him a knowing wink. "You have a third gift, Franklin. I'm not sure you quite know how much you're loved…by everyone in this room."

"What's this?" Wheezy asked, leaning *The Dancing Boy* against the sofa cushion. "This old guy can't take any more."

Dillon removed the paper. As the illuminated face emerged, Wheezy broke into a broad smile. He touched the cool canvas as if it glowed hot beneath his fingers. With a questioning gaze, he addressed Mary.

"In this portrait, you're looking at something. Your thoughts seem so far away."

Mary turned and pointed to *The Dancing Boy*. "Over the bed in Richmond is Dillon's copy of this painting; the original now sits right here. At the moment Dillon snapped my picture for the portrait, I was wishing that I'd brought the *The Dancing Boy* home to Portland after I made Doc immortal. I always regretted that I didn't bring it back with me. I got my wish." Mary embraced Wheezy. "Art and music, Franklin. Your life is full, and now…so is mine."

"I'll hang *The Dancing Boy* and your portrait on opposite walls of the bedroom to complete the meaning. You'll be able to look at it all the time." Wheezy whispered in her ear, but everyone heard him, anyway: "*Your* portrait is going over *our* bed."

CHAPTER 27

Autumn Leaves

This particular autumn produced spectacular foliage. Warm afternoons and frosty evenings in September were a precise recipe for setting the maple trees on fire with color. This was a perfect Saturday for holding Legs's memorial celebration. Jean hadn't been able to let go of her and Spence's need for closure and had finally convinced Wheezy to do an informal gathering at the store after closing time. Nothing big: only a meaningful installation of Legs's ashes in his hutch that held his other mementos, including the harmonica. Plus, the store would be closed on Sunday. They could sleep in if they celebrated too much.

Today, Wiley and Mycroft missed their chance for a ride in the T-Bird. As they had on most days over the past month, both immortal animals preferred wreaking havoc at Not Fade Away in their attempt to "help" Spence and Bill. Of course, only those two men could see the resident troublemakers. Their invisibility prompted quizzical stares from customers when Spence scolded the two for knocking down displays, batting the buttons on the cash drawer, and generally getting under foot. Wiley had been known to pull on the bags to prevent customers from leaving the store. Bill calmed nerves by saying Spence had some mental backlash from his bad behavior in the sixties. Bill hadn't been half wrong.

Jean pulled the car into a space around the corner from the store. Per Wheezy's request, she'd brought Legs's urn and six meatball submarine sandwiches from Shut Up and Eat in Southeast Portland, not too far away. The celebration had turned into an all-day affair: Legs's music playing throughout the day; a signing event filled the afternoon; and a private submarine sandwich party would start after the store's closing. Jean hoped Jon and Dan would get away from work to join the fun.

Out of habit, Jean peered into the window of the antiques collective on the corner. It had been decorated with a Halloween theme; vines of silk leaves in autumn colors circled the vintage toys, vases, and figurines stacked on three levels. She did a double take at the long box standing upright on the second tier of the display.

"Oh my God!" she said, immediately turning around to check if anyone had overheard her. She stepped inside the store. The bell above the door tinkled in the quiet shop. The woodsy aroma of aging books and dinged furniture escorted her into the world of heirlooms. The glass-fronted cases were stuffed with costume jewelry and small decorative items that meant something uniquely special to the original owners but would create future memories in a continued life with a new one.

"Hello. Need any help?" an elderly man muttered from behind yesterday's copy of the *Oregonian*. From his girth, he wasn't planning on helping with anything.

"Yes. I think so."

"Whatcha got?" The shopkeeper snapped the newspaper and folded it in half. The chair squeaked as he leaned on the counter, but he didn't move to get up.

Jean pointed to the front window. "Can you show me the tall box next to the Lionel train set?"

The man stared at her, almost surprised. "How'd you spot that? Just put it in the window this mornin'.'"

"Caught my eye, I guess."

Jean stepped to the display and waved for the man to join her. With great effort, he limped from behind the counter and puffed toward her, already out of breath. He leaned over the fuzzy pumpkins and a caboose.

"Yes, that yellow one."

"Some old man was waitin' with it when I opened the shop this morning," he said, handing her the box. "Never seen him before. Told me to put it in the window 'cause I'd sell it today. I'll be damned if he wasn't right. I can tell you're gonna buy it."

Jean started to laugh but went quiet. Inside the cellophane cover was a fifteen-inch doll dressed in Levis and a blue-checked shirt. A smiling Legs stared at her from behind black sunglasses. He even had a harmonica accessory set in the molded plastic casing. The toy's title was Action Jazz Series, with *Action Legs* written diagonally in red along the bottom of the box. She suspected who that "old man" was.

"I'll take it. Do you have an *Action Wheezy* too?" she asked, trying to keep a straight face.

"A what? I didn't even know about this one. Must be pretty rare. I heard of Legs Flanders. *Real* famous," he said, nodding. "Fellow down the street has a bunch of his records. I think they was friends."

"How much?"

Jean studied the man as he rubbed the gray stubble on his chin, clearly assessing the limit on her credit card. With every scratchy swipe, the price went up.

"A legend. Didn't he pass away not too long ago?"

"Yes, but—"

"Makes it more valuable." He hesitated and met her gaze. "Fifty bucks?"

"Sold!" Jean beamed and ran her finger along the top of the urn with Legs's ashes. "Legends don't die, by the way, so add a hundred to the total."

The man's eyes widened. "You made my day, young lady."

"No one's called me that in thirty years. You just made mine too."

As Jean signed the credit card slip, one she'd tuck away for safekeeping, the man dug around beneath the counter.

"This is the only one that'll fit a box that long," he said, handing her the large hemp-handled shopping bag. She set the urn inside with the action figure and stepped toward the door. With her hand on the handle and the sandwiches dangling in the bag from her wrist, she stopped and turned.

"Did the old man say anything else?"

"Nope," the shopkeeper said, shaking his head. "But now I think I shoulda charged you five hundred bucks."

"Any price wouldn't have been too high." The bell tinkled. "Thank you! I'll stop in again."

Stepping outside, Jean stood and closed her eyes. With the bright sun warming her face, she appreciated life's little surprises, meaningless to others but priceless to her. The fall breeze stilled as a voice gave her a start.

"Thought I'd make a contribution to the celebration. You can't resist looking in that window, am I right, Jean?"

She recognized the Southern drawl and turned. Doc leaned against the brick edge of the shop's entrance, appearing smug. "But how?"

"Oh, I still have a few tricks tucked up my sleeve. Found a fella who makes prototypes of toys. What did Ella tell Legs on her photo? Yes, *Keep on Running.*"

"Never stop running, Doc."

"Glad I ran into you."

"Talk like that will sweep a girl off her feet," she said, shading her eyes.

"Go on, now. I believe Wheezy needs his meatballs." Doc gave her a two-fingered salute, adjusted his hat, and disappeared.

"Doc, you are the limit."

She bounced on air toward Not Fade Away. The vibrant red leaves dropped from the maple trees lining the path. They swirled behind her.

A *bing-bong* sounded above the door as Jean stepped inside Not Fade Away. In honor of Legs's ad hoc memorial service, Dexter Gordon's "I Guess I'll Hang My Tears Out To Dry" was on the day's playlist. The aisles teemed with collectors flipping through the stacks. Their fingers slowed as the haunting sax tune filled the air. The shop had been designed to have the appearance of being in business for thirty years, but Bill and Spence didn't skimp on the modern sound system. They'd created a friendly place for vinylphiles to hang out, swap concert memories, and listen to music. Spence even had note cards printed with bits of colorful trivia and scandalous anecdotes on them. They were added to the bags at the cash register.

"Closing in ten minutes, Spence," Jean warned, patting the glass counter at the cash register. "You guys need to get all these people out."

"What time is it? I lost track." Spence slipped a trivia note card in a paper bag and handed it to a young woman with neon-pink spiky hair. This one said: *The first jazz recording was performed by New Orleans' own The Original Dixieland Jazz Band in 1917.*

"Almost six. We're starting right on the hour." She craned her neck to see Wheezy and Dillon in the back. She held up the bag of sandwiches and started down the aisle, but had to lean to the side to let Mycroft run by with Wiley close on his tail.

Wheezy had taken up his usual place at a built-in counter specially constructed for personal appearances and signings with local musicians. A stack of albums from Legs's collection sat in front of him, along with a line of fans snaking almost to the tiki section. Next to him, Dillon inspected the cover of a Miles Davis album and then handed it to Wheezy for his signature.

The new owner marched right to the cash register after Wheezy added his flowing script: *Wheezy Beevers for the Legs Flanders Collection.*

Wheezy stood and raised his hands when he spotted Jean coming toward him.

"Subs! Come to Daddy! You went to Shut Up and Eat?" he shouted.

"Yep. We have to wait until the store's empty. Ten minutes before we close. Sign as many as you can to whittle down this line." Shimmying to the storeroom in the back corner for napkins and plastic utensils, she waved for Spence to join her.

"What's up? It's really busy," Spence said.

"Look."

Jean pulled out the urn. Spence wrapped his hands around it as if it were a prized Egyptian artifact, admiring the floating musical phrase circling the rim.

"This is going in Legs's locked case." Spence moved to part the curtains to the sales floor.

"Wait. One more thing…from Doc." Jean showed him the long box.

"Hilarious!"

Turning it over, she pointed to the back: a brief and tender tribute to Legs.

Born in Mississippi in 1929, Lawrence "Legs" Flanders had only one dream that guided his life: to be a musician. Both he and his music stood tall above the crowd. As a boy, the harmonica was his instrument of choice. But it was his horn that drew history's greats to Legs's talent, including Louis Armstrong, John Coltrane, Dizzy Gillespie, Ella Fitzgerald, and the singular Franklin "Wheezy" Beevers. His life ended as it began . . . with the magic of a harmonica.

"Where did you get this?"

"At the corner antiques collective. Doc put this box in the

window. He knew we wanted to make the mood light for the party. When I left the store, he was waiting for me." She set her hand on Spence's arm. "I think this was his way of making Legs immortal for us."

Spence didn't say a word. He carried both prized items toward the locked display cabinet that held Legs's treasures. He pulled the original two keys, tied with twine, from his pocket and slipped one in the lock. The urn went on the middle shelf; the box was set on the top one to accommodate the height. Plucking a Not Fade Away business card from his breast pocket, he gazed at store's logo of the three phoenixes. He wrote *Not for Sale* on the back and rested it against the box.

She lined up the meatball sandwiches and plenty of napkins, on the counter.

"Got to close on time tonight, everybody!" Bill called out. "Having a private event here tonight. Sorry! Wheezy Beevers will be back on Monday."

Linda waited at the entrance as the customers reluctantly streamed out, many of whom wanted to participate in the celebration. After the last forlorn face exited, Linda locked the door. She turned to the group.

"One. Two. Three. *Pour!*"

Wheezy pulled the preselected album out of the sleeve and placed the thick disk on the turntable. He blew on the tone arm and lowered the needle. The store filled with Art Tatum's version of "Over the Rainbow."

Spence pulled eight vintage shot glasses from Legs's cabinet and lined them up on the signing counter. He poured Fortaleza tequila into six of them—no one at that party was going to deny Dillon a drink just because he wasn't yet twenty-one.

"Why eight glasses?" Bill asked.

"Dan and Jon might join us, but let's get started."

Each glass bore the name of a club where Legs had played. Jean selected the shot glass from the Triple Door; Spence picked up the Blue Note.

"To our dear friend Legs. May he live forever!" Spence announced.

The clinks produced no tears, no shattered wishes, only hopes for a future with Legs in their hearts. They tossed back the shots in sequence and slammed the glasses on the counter.

Wheezy shivered at the burn and pulled down the wrapping on his sandwich. He wandered—a bit unsteady—to the cabinet, staged exactly as it had been in Legs's living room in DC. He scanned the shelves of remaining mementos: guitar picks, Louis Armstrong's handkerchief and, of course, the famous harmonica. He lingered the longest on the urn.

"Ashes to ashes. Meatball or bust," he announced and held up the sub. He took a big bite. Wheezy's gaze rose to the box with the action doll. As he turned and stared at the group, a blop of tomato sauce dribbled down the front of his V-neck yellow sweater.

"What the hell?"

"A gift from Doc," Jean said. "He wanted to contribute to the fun. He has an unusual sense of humor."

Bill stepped to the case and started laughing. "Where's the Wheezy one?" he asked. "Says they're a series."

"I have no doubt we'll have a short, wide box next to Legs at some point. But we're not there yet." Jean snatched several napkins from the counter and handed them to Wheezy.

"You have me on preorder?" Wheezy blinked from behind his magnifiers.

"Release date to be determined," Spence added, splashing one more round of tequila in the line of shot glasses.

"Actionnnn…jaaazzz. I'd better write a theme song." Wheezy's eyes twinkled with a tune already coming together in his head. "On second thought, tell Doc I want to be a Wheezy bobblehead."

Jean heard three car doors thump outside. She turned to the

picture window by the entrance. Beyond the laminated newspaper article with the headline "Amazing Light Show at
Milwaukie Jazz Festival" in the front window, a black Crown
Victoria had parked in the one-hour zone. Dan and Jon stepped
out of the driver's and passenger side. A large man exited from
the backseat. The chief—with two records in his hand. Jean
followed their path to the door. Jon tried the handle and then
knocked on the glass. Linda rushed to the front door and turned
the key to let them in.

"Fill three more shot glasses!" she called out.

Jean leaned down to Wheezy's ear. "I wish I had a nickel for
every time you and Legs said that. I think the chief wants your
autograph."

Wheezy beamed and marched to the front of the store.
"Well, if it isn't the two little *G*s and the big cheese!" He stuck
out his hand to the chief. "Wheezy Beevers. I hear you're a big
fan. Gimme your pen. I'll sign your albums."

CHAPTER 28

*Stitches, Brushes, and Riffs…*We're Immortal

By Halloween, yet another new normal settled over the Collins household. Wiley called dibs on the bottom of the bed; Mycroft hogged the space between Jean and Spence. Wheezy spent his evenings with Mary, but nothing could tear him away from Not Fade Away during the days. Spence had to admit, Wheezy kept the customers coming in the door and loaded down with albums on their way out. Plus, Wheezy was fond of the chicken-and-asparagus enchiladas from Casa de Tamales down the street from the record store. Cooking wasn't on Wheezy's to-do list. If the meal didn't come from a restaurant, then it needed to *ding* when hot. Spence and Bill were endlessly entertained when Wheezy hopped into his pin-striped smart car and zipped back to Irvington each evening.

Jean had a new project, and it was taking shape fast. For the past few months, she'd spent her days on the phone going over the details of production and fund-raising. Only Spence was in on the developments. A surprise.

She flipped through the mail and pulled out a thick envelope from Landrum & Sullivan. Tossing the rest of the stack aside, she opened it and perused the seventy pages packed in a black clip. Over her twenty years of management, mergers, acquisitions, and self-inflicted (sometimes) stress, she'd never accomplished anything close to what these papers contained. She set them on the kitchen island

and stared, scrolling through images of all that had happened since she and Spence moved from Houston. They had fulfilled the magic's summons to help many people. Mary said that Wheezy's life had been made full with his art and music. Well, her and Spence's lives were full too. Spence opened his record store; she would manage this. In fact, the first project was already underway.

Jean stepped to the den and retrieved the special pen Spence had given her late in her corporate career from its stand on the desk. As she passed through the living room, she stopped and stood at Doc's portrait. With the immortal animals on their bed upstairs, an audience of one—a wise one—sat in front of her.

"We're going to do what we talked about in Richmond, Doc," she announced to the canvas. No response came from the painting, only a long gaze filled with simple answers to difficult questions. She shook herself back into the moment, the pen in her hand reminding her of the original mission.

At the kitchen island, Jean sat and signed her name—page after page—at each color-coded sticky tab. Spence had his own lines to sign. She raced through the last two pages when she heard the Mini Cooper pull into the garage.

"Guess what's here?" she called out as the mudroom door opened.

Spence slipped off his sneakers, without untying them, and stepped into the kitchen in his white gym socks.

"I can only imagine. I take that back...I *can't* imagine."

"We're immortal." Jean handed him the stack of pages from Landrum & Sullivan. "All looks good; every point we discussed with Don Landrum is covered. All the *T*'s are crossed and *I*'s dotted."

"This is really happening," he said, his chest heaving with breath. "When's the first one?"

"Mid-December of next year. The actual date is moving around. The interviews are getting scheduled. They're in preproduction now. A crew is on its way to Cairo to document every step with Anhur for the second one. The FBI is another matter. We're bogged down in the approval process."

"Did you sign?"

"Yep. Just waiting for your John Hancock, Mr. Collins. The proceeds from Mary's house are doing good work."

"Has the funding been approved from the Cairo and the Portland museums too?"

"Just waiting for the paperwork. I have the verbal thumbs up."

She handed him the special pen. "They're going to use the program to promote the exhibit so the expense is considered part of their marketing budget. Less red tape."

Spence poised his hand over the first page. "This will keep you out of trouble."

"But magic and mischief always lead to something good."

It took nearly a year from the signing of those documents for Jean and Spence to realize the fruits of their commitment. The goal was to create immortality a different way—no magic. Highlighting the accomplishments of those who brought magic to other people's lives seemed to be enough. The quest to deliver something special was more than a full-time job for the board members: Jean, Spence, and Wheezy. Everything needed to be approved and funded—film crews, travel arrangements, production details—in the quest to deliver something special. And tonight was the first of many something-specials.

The week after Thanksgiving, Jean and Spence raced to put up the twelve-foot noble fir and finish the inside decorations for the party. For the outside they blew up brightly colored beach balls and wrapped each in four feet of cellophane. They hung them from the eaves on the front of the house. The effect, when lit from the ground, resembled oversize hard candies. The neighbors called the Collinses' the Candy House every Christmastime.

The Candy House was full tonight with beings in various stages of living. With a drying towel over her shoulder, Jean sat on the top step overlooking the living room. Bill and Linda had kicked her out of the kitchen so they could finish the dishes.

Doc, Charlotte, Birdie, and Jess sat in chairs around the fireplace. Charlotte, Doc's wife, wasn't comfortable with traveling through space for long distances but made an exception for tonight. She didn't want to miss the big event. Plus, in her demure way, she caught everyone up on the gossip about visitors to the inn in Richmond. Doc was looking forward to hosting the chief and his wife at the Old Gaines House. They'd already booked their dates for the spring.

Wheezy and Mary sank into the pillows, hand in hand, on the loveseat. Wheezy's stockinged feet rested on the hassock as he munched on popcorn from the bowl in his lap. Doc eyed the pair, unable to put aside his status as the approving father. A slight smile hinted at his elation for Mary's fortune to have a good man by her immortal side.

Jon Segert and his wife, Meg, sat next to Dan on the opposite couch. Meg crowed about how happy she was to have the talon out of their life. Like Lady Diana, she said there "wasn't room for three of us in this marriage." Having never met the immortals, except through Jon's descriptions, Meg couldn't stop glancing at them and nervously tucking her long brown hair behind her ears. Jean figured Meg had better get used to it because an offer was forthcoming to come on board as fund-raiser.

Dan Brick brought his fiancée, Christine. He'd proposed—again—shortly after Legs's memorial party. Jean helped him pick out the ring, a simple heirloom rose-cut center stone with two side baguettes in a platinum setting. After significant prepping, Dan was relieved that Christine seemed so at ease with the group. Her fascination with Wiley prompted a nudge that they really should adopt their own immortal dog after the wedding on Valentine's Day.

"Just think. We'll never have to go through the loss of a pet," Christine suggested.

"We'll see, sweetheart. One step at a time." Dan kissed her fingers.

"Be forewarned. They're high maintenance," Spence advised, "but pretty irresistible. No trips to the vet and you can take them anywhere."

Dillon sprawled in front of the fireplace with Mycroft, studying the radiating haze around his form. The Mycroft painting was over the fireplace, showing his illuminated form leaping after the three phoenixes in flight. Even though fairly small, one foot by two, Dillon had used every color of the rainbow in the vivid painting. The title was *Mycroft's Release*. The cat was flying like a feline angel.

"The more I look at the Mycroft painting the happier I am with the way it came out," he said.

"It's perfect," Jean crowed. "In fact, when I showed it to Palmer at the museum he wanted it for the collection." She made a playful snap of the kitchen towel on Dillon's stocking feet. "Of course, I said no."

It was a treat for her and Spence to have Dillon staying with them for the holidays. They hadn't been ready when he left for Washington, DC, but time marched forward whether she and Spence liked it or not. The sting had been soothed by the way she had chosen to keep tabs on him. Getting approval from the FBI to film a documentary of his first year of sleuthing hadn't been easy, but Jon had greased the skids. The final decision had gone all the way to the top echelon of the FBI. The project was a go and would be shown to a wide audience. The FBI was okay with that because it would use the film for training and publicity purposes. By this time next year, the world would learn of Dillon's talent and skill.

"Did I hear you're working on your first big case, Dillon?" Jon asked.

"A Sherlock Holmes, he is," Birdie interjected, crossing her thick arms. "Huntin' things is dangerous. Liable to get killed with his own gun. I don't like it one bit."

"They won't let nothin' happen to him, Birdie," Jess said, reassuring her. "I'll make sure-a that." Jess tipped his head to Jon.

Dillon now had a Horus-like protector of his own looking out for him.

"I can't talk too much about it at this stage." Dillon rolled over to face the group and propped himself up on his elbow. "But I can tell you stolen art from the Nazi era is pouring into the market. I'm working on a case that's just surfaced. People are getting old enough and want to sell them off. Medical bills and taxes will push a lot of stuff off the walls and into the light. I'll be authenticating them. Amazing art is going back to the museums and families who were stolen from in the thirties and forties. What goes around eventually comes around."

"Good work. Important work," Jon agreed. "And thank you for the compliment, Jess. Dillon's on the research side, Birdie, not the shooting side. He doesn't carry a gun."

"Wars don't seem to end, Mr. Segert." Birdie shook her head. "I don't want *nothin'* to happen to this boy."

Dillon scratched Mycroft's chin and admired his luminous, cinnamon-patched face. "This is important too. I miss this little guy."

"Your talent will get you through anything," Jean said. "You'll always be with us. I wouldn't be surprised if you start getting regular visits from both Mycroft and Wiley. And don't forget, you still have to paint. Spence, are you ready? Five-minute warning." Dillon's documentary, yet to be filmed, of course, was just part of a bigger project, and they had all gathered together to witness the debut of their efforts.

"All set." Spence fiddled with the television, double- and triple-checking the timer menu for recording the program. He backed away and rubbed his hands together.

After finishing the dishes, Bill and Linda joined the group, carrying two chairs to the living room. Of all the people who had shared their journey, the Flannerys had been with them from the beginning. This was an important moment that wouldn't have happened without them.

"I wish Anhur could have been here to see this," Jon said.

Dan raised his hand. "I second that."

"No worries." Spence set the remote on the hassock next to Wheezy's feet. "I e-mailed him. PBS is streaming this on the Internet, and the series will be coming out on DVD in May."

"Did you remind Jan and Doug Parson back in Richmond?" Jean asked.

"Yes, dear. I called the first time you reminded me."

Jean sat in the leather club chair next to Spence. Mycroft trotted to her and jumped in her lap, kicking up a dusting of ignited static that floated down the legs of her black slacks. He turned in a circle and set his head over her knees. Wiley abandoned Christine's petting hand to settle at Doc's feet.

"We made this happen, honey," Spence said.

"We certainly did." Jean smacked her hand on his in a high five.

"*Shhh*. You two, put a cork in it," Wheezy chided, swishing his hands. "We're starting." He set the bowl of popcorn on the floor and grasped Mary's hand.

Meg reached out for Jon's hand, gazing at him with pride. She turned to the television.

Out of all the auditions for the program's host, Jean insisted the introduction be delivered by Jon Segert: stoic, tender, articulate, and loyal friend. The perfect choice. Sitting on the same stool that Legs had graced on the stage at the festival, Jon lifted one loafer to the bottom rung with his hands laced in his lap. He looked dapper in a navy-blue V-neck sweater and butter-yellow cotton shirt. His crew cut was freshly buzzed. His smooth voice silenced the chatter in the crowded living room.

Doc glanced at Jean. He tipped his head in immortal approval as their eyes met. His illuminated hand covered Charlotte's as he lowered his head and listened.

"Tonight we're proud to premiere a new series: *Immortal Legends*. We'll examine the quiet heroes who have impacted the lives of others, from those who are gone from us but never forgotten, as well as legends of the future. We'll tell of a country doctor, Dr. Beaumont Gaines, who helped countless citizens in Richmond, Virginia, at the end of the Civil War and two jazz musicians who changed the face of music. We'll follow the career of a gifted young painter turned sleuth, Dillon Davis, who works with the FBI to find stolen art. And finally, we'll record the painstaking process of assembling the artifacts of Nefertari's tomb with the director of the Cairo Museum, Anhur Kumar, for the upcoming exhibition with the Portland Museum of Art. But tonight, we open the series with the life of jazz legend Legs Flanders: poet laureate in music, explorer of the new, and visionary in his time."

The lilting and tender notes of the piano started the opening theme, a lyrical and classical version of Steve Earle's "Transcendental Blues," arranged and performed by Wheezy. The song was selected by Spence, who said the artist was a legend and poet in his own right.

"My song!" Wheezy exclaimed, pointing to the speakers. "Did that in one take in the studio."

Mary patted his hand. "Of course you did, dear."

A logo appeared in the center of the screen: two paw prints with an illuminated outline—one petite, the other substantial—set inside an endless, reflective gold circle.

"Hey, those prints are from Croft Man and Sparkles! Nice," Bill said, nodding his head in approval.

"Here it comes…" Jean said. A tingle filled her hand as she smoothed down the everlasting fur on Mycroft's back. She hadn't been embarrassed by her tears in the sound booth when the technician declared the final take to be "the one." She listened for the rich voice that filled her life with light.

Spence's voice.

"Funding for this program is made possible by the generous support of the Wiley-Mycroft Foundation and from viewers like you."

AUTHOR'S NOTE

There's nothing like setting down the needle on vintage vinyl. The snaps and pops provided endless inspiration for celebrating jazz artists and their indelible music. I listened to a lot of great tunes while writing this book. My husband, Wayne, is a wonderful teacher. I learned so much about the colorful lives of those who took music in a whole new direction. The genius of the numerous artists I mention in the book, including, Muddy Waters, Art Tatum, Jon Coltrane, Ella Fitzgerald, Ethyl Waters, Herb Ellis, Willie Dixon, Fats Waller, Bix Biederbeck, Louis Armstrong, and Dizzy Gillespie will never be repeated.

When local businesses make an impact on my community, I like to support their growth by incorporating them into the story. In particular, Casa de Tamales, Portofino Restaurant, Shut Up and Eat, Music Millennium, and the Milwaukie Farmer's Market deserve those accolades.

The Portland Museum of Art is a fictional museum in the book. The real one, the Portland Art Museum, is an important gem in the cultural landscape of the city. Maybe one day, we really will get an exhibit of Nefertari's treasures. For now, though, it is a wish that comes true in fiction.

I chose financial cheats and inside traders for my antagonists in all three books of the trilogy because they are the killers of dreams. The charges against my character, Anthony Dromov, are the exact ones rendered against Bernie Madoff. As of this writing, the Madoff Ponzi scheme is the most damaging in history, not only to its direct victims but to the trust the public has in the entire financial system.

Legs Flanders and Wheezy Beevers are purely fictional characters. Little bits and pieces of their souls, though, came from all the legendary musicians mentioned in the book. The magical harmonica once owned by Muddy Waters is only a wish in the breeze, the product of vivid imagination.

Legends never die as long as we remember them.

ABOUT THE AUTHOR

Courtney Pierce lives in Milwaukie, Oregon, with her husband and bossy cat. *Stitches, Brushes,* and *Riffs* emerged from her own magical history, which encompassed a twenty-year career as an executive in the Broadway entertainment industry. She became transformed by the magic of fiction from a theater seat in thirty-two cities for touring Broadway shows. Her short story, *1313 Huidekoper Place*, was selected for inclusion in the 2013 *NIWA Short Story Anthology of Speculative Fiction*. Courtney is active in the writing community. She has completed the Hawthorne Fellows program at the Attic Institute and is Vice President of the Northwest Independent Writers Association.

Follow the *Stitches* trilogy at Courtney's website and blog:
www.courtney-pierce.com
www.stitchesthenovel.blogspot.com

Courtney's next book, *The Executrix*, is due out in 2015.

Made in the USA
Coppell, TX
03 September 2021

61717180R00132